"Kiss me, Quenby," Gunner commanded with a coaxing smile.

"Why should I? I'm furious with you," she said.

"Because I want it so much I feel as if I'm dying." He stood only a breath away. "It hurts me when you're angry with me. Do you want me to show you how I'm hurting?"

"I'm hurting too." She looked at him then and saw that he knew. He smelled of soap, maple leaves, and sunlight, and the heat emitting from his body was wrapping her in a spellbinding web of feelings she couldn't escape.

"Let's help each other, love," he said. Then his lips touched hers, not moving, but waiting.

She gave a broken little cry deep in her throat. "Oh, Gunner, I think I hate you."

"No, you don't." He was pressing hot, urgent kisses on her cheeks and throat. "You love me. That's what this is all about. But don't worry. No one could love you more than I do."

She felt a wild, primitive thrill in that moment, a savage satisfaction in his words. Then all she felt was his mouth on hers. . . .

WHAT ARE *LOVESWEPT* ROMANCES?

They are stories of true romance and touching emotion. We believe those two very important ingredients are constants in our highly sensual and very believable stories in the *LOVESWEPT* line. Our goal is to give you, the reader, stories of consistently high quality that may sometimes make you laugh, sometimes make you cry, but are always fresh and creative and contain many delightful surprises within their pages.

Most romance fans read an enormous number of books. Those they truly love, they keep. Others may be traded with friends and soon forgotten. We hope that each *LOVESWEPT* romance will be a treasure—a "keeper." We will always try to publish

LOVE STORIES YOU'LL NEVER FORGET
BY AUTHORS YOU'LL ALWAYS REMEMBER

The Editors

LOVESWEPT® • 232

Iris Johansen
Star Light, Star Bright

BANTAM BOOKS
TORONTO • NEW YORK • LONDON • SYDNEY • AUCKLAND

STAR LIGHT, STAR BRIGHT

A Bantam Book / January 1988

LOVESWEPT® and the wave device are registered trademarks of Bantam Books, Inc. Registered in U.S. Patent and Trademark Office and elsewhere.

If you would be interested in receiving protective vinyl covers for your Loveswept books, please write to this address for information:

Loveswept
Bantam Books
P.O. Box 985
Hicksville, NY 11802

ISBN 0-553-21861-1

Published simultaneously in the United States and Canada

Bantam Books are published by Bantam Books, Inc. Its trademark, consisting of the words "Bantam Books" and the portrayal of a rooster, is Registered in U.S. Patent and Trademark Office and in other countries. Marca Registrada. Bantam Books, Inc., 666 Fifth Avenue, New York, New York 10103.

PRINTED IN THE UNITED STATES OF AMERICA

O   0 9 8 7 6 5 4 3 2 1

One

"Will he be all right?" Elizabeth whispered. Tears glittered in her eyes as she watched the Lear jet taxi down the runway. "Oh, Jon, I don't want him to go."

Jon's arm swiftly encircled her waist in a gesture of love and support. "I know you don't. Neither do I." He cleared his throat. "You could have said no. The Clanad left it up to you. They recommended, but you decided. I could still call a council meeting and tell them you've changed your mind, that you think it's the wrong solution."

"I just don't know." Elizabeth watched the Lear jet lift into the sky and slowly turned away. "Andrew's only five. Perhaps we should have allowed him more time."

"It would only have gotten worse," Jon said

gently. "We want him healthy and free, don't we, love?"

"Oh, yes." Elizabeth smiled shakily. "I just wish I could be there to help him."

"You love him too much."

"He's my son. Of course I love him." Elizabeth blinked back the tears. "And he's so special, Jon. So loving and beautiful and . . ." She shook her head. "I'm being a typical mother, aren't I? I know it will be all right. Gunner will watch over him." She made a face. "Or maybe Andrew will watch over Gunner. Sometimes I'm not sure who's the child and who's the adult. Perhaps that nanny can keep them both in order. She sounds very sensible."

"Quite sensible." A curious smile touched Jon's lips. "And I'm sure you're right about Quenby Swensen. I think she'll be a very stabilizing influence on both Andrew and Gunner."

"Why are you smiling? Is there something I should know?"

"Only that the Clanad made some interesting projections regarding Quenby Swensen after they investigated her. She may be—" He stopped and then shrugged his shoulders. "But you're not interested in their genetic studies. I remember you were quite indignant when I told you what a wonderful match we were going to be." His dark eyes twinkled. "Even though their predictions proved absolutely correct."

Her eyes widened. "Does Gunner know?"

"Certainly. He's on the governing board of the

Clanad and has access to all information. He was intrigued. Not convinced, but definitely interested."

"Heaven help Quenby Swensen." Elizabeth sighed. "I wouldn't want to try to tame a wild Scaramouche like Gunner. He may be the most lovable man in this hemisphere, perhaps in the world, but it would drive me insane worrying about what he was going to do next."

"But Quenby Swensen enjoys a challenge. That's one of the reasons she was chosen to take care of Andrew." Jon took her elbow and began propelling her toward the chauffeured limousine waiting at the side of the tarmac. "And you're not so bad at taking on challenges yourself, love. You married me."

"And never regretted it," Elizabeth added. "Not for a minute." She glanced over her shoulder, but the Learjet was lost to sight. "We *are* doing the right thing, aren't we Jon? He's so little, and life hasn't been easy for him."

"I know." He opened the door of the limousine for her. "It will never be easy for him; he's too much like you." His gaze gravely met hers. "But we can try to make it better; we can try to make him whole. Gunner has made all the arrangements. All we can do now is wait."

"Wait . . ." Elizabeth knew it was going to be a long, tense period even with Jon supporting her. "Well, at least Andrew will be able to live at Mill Cottage for a few months, even if I'm not with him. I've always wanted him to see my old home. Where is this Swensen woman supposed to join them?"

"The Learjet is picking her up in Zarbondal.

She's just resigned a position caring for the son of the prime minister." He grimaced. "I'd say she was leaving just in time. I understand the government is collapsing and the members of the cabinet are running for their lives. She'll probably be grateful for the tranquility of Mill Cottage after the last two years. Zarbondal has been a hotbed of turmoil during her entire stay there."

"Why didn't she leave?"

"The child needed her." Jon met her gaze. "He was deaf and had withdrawn into an almost catatonic state."

Elizabeth stiffened. "And she helped him?"

"She helped him. He's adjusting very well now." Jon leaned forward and kissed her lightly on the lips. "And she'll help Andrew too. She's a strong, sensitive woman. Trust her."

"I'm going to try." She leaned back against him, loving the solid warmth and security of his muscular body, loving *him*. If he trusted Quenby Swensen, then she must trust her too. She knew Jon loved Andrew as much as she did and wanted only the best for him. "I just hope she knows what she's getting herself into. What did you tell her when you offered her the position?"

"Nothing much. I left it to Gunner's discretion."

"Discretion? Gunner?" She slowly shook her head. "The poor woman is in for a rude shock."

The man had to be totally mad.

Quenby was mesmerized with horror as she gazed out the window at the tall man dashing across the tarmac, dodging a spate of machine-gun bullets from the two men on the roof of the terminal building. He had to be crazy to take chances like this.

She had watched the white Learjet land against orders from the guerrillas holding the control tower and then take off again, leaving the golden-haired man standing alone on the runway. She had known he had no chance, that he was going to be killed before he reached the terminal, shot down before her eyes. Incredibly, not one bullet had touched him . . . yet. He was zigzagging, dodging bullets as a matador would dodge a bull's sharp horns, finding protection behind baggage trucks and fork lifts until he finally reached the door of the terminal.

He flung open the door, sending it smashing against the wall. He was out of breath, his white-gold hair disheveled, a smear of oil on the knee of his jeans. His blue eyes were shining with excitement and vitality as they searched the crowd. He was quite probably the most handsome man she had ever seen. His good-looking features were set off by a deep tan, and his fair hair shimmered under the rays of the late afternoon sun streaming through the windows of the terminal. Dressed in jeans and a black leather flight jacket, his tall, slim body appeared arousingly tough and muscular. "Quenby Swensen?" he shouted. "Is Quenby Swensen here?"

Oh, no, it couldn't be . . . The agency had said Jon Sandell would send a man to pick her up and share the guardianship of his son for the summer, but surely it couldn't be this reckless daredevil. "Yes." She stepped forward. "I'm Quenby Swensen."

"Gunner Nilsen." He started to cut his way through the crowd toward her. "I was sent to pick you up and take you to Albany. I was hoping you'd still be here. I thought maybe the prime minister had decided to take you with him when he and his family fled the country."

She shook her head. "They left the country last night with the rest of the cabinet. None of the staff were permitted on the flight."

Gunner frowned. "They just left you here, with the whole country going up in flames?" He stopped before her. "With the airport closed and held by the revolutionaries?"

"The airport wasn't closed last night. The revolutionaries took it over just a few hours ago," she answered defensively. "No one realized I'd be in any danger if I waited another day."

"If they had any brains in their head, they had to know there was a chance of your being hurt or captured," he said dryly. "Your former employers don't seem overly concerned about your welfare."

"They were afraid," she said simply. "They're good people, but their lives were falling apart around them. You can't blame people for being afraid under those circumstances." She added deliberately, "Only crazy people risk their lives. I never saw anything so foolhardy in my life as you running across that tarmac. Why did your plane land when the tower must have told you the airport was closed?"

His sapphire-blue eyes twinkled. "I'm only a humble employee like yourself and I was told to stop here and pick up Quenby Swensen. No one said anything about dropping the pickup if the airport was closed. I just had to operate on my own initiative."

Humble employee? Quenby had an idea there was nothing humble about Gunner Nilsen, and she doubted if any "employee" would have the authority to risk a Learjet worth a small fortune on a reckless whim. "Well, it was very stupid," she said bluntly. "You could have been killed for no good reason."

His smile faded as he studied her face. "And do you always have to have a good reason for everything you do?"

"I try to be sensible," Quenby said. "I was brought up to recognize the practicalities of life."

A brilliant smile lit the bronze darkness of his face. "Perhaps you recognize them, but I think you ignore them on occasion," he said softly. "Why else would you be stranded in the middle of a revolution? There must be safer positions open to a woman of your qualifications."

She felt a strange breathlessness, and she had to force herself to pull her gaze away from his. "There's a big difference between being involved in danger through no fault of one's own and sheer recklessness. Why didn't you have the Learjet pull closer to the terminal so that you didn't have all that distance to run?"

"My godchild, Andrew, is aboard the plane," Gunner said. "I may take chances with my own life but never with anyone else's. I wanted the jet out of range of those machine guns when it took off."

"I see."

"Are those two men with machine guns up on the roof the only sentries here?" Gunner asked.

She nodded. "The revolutionaries took control of the tower but they mounted only the one armed position. They haven't bothered any of the passengers in the terminal building. Their goal seems to be the preventing of takeoffs and landings."

"Is that your only suitcase?" He nodded to the canvas tote on the floor beside her.

"No, I have two suitcases in a locker. I sent the rest of my luggage several days ago to the address my agency gave me. Why?"

"Can you manage them by yourself?"

She nodded.

"Get them and meet me at the departure door." He glanced at his watch. "The Learjet will be landing in ten minutes and we want to be ready."

"Are you completely insane? I have no intention of racing across those runways trying to dodge a hail of bullets."

He smiled. "I wouldn't think of putting a lady in such an undignified position. There won't be any bullets and I'll even borrow one of those baggage trucks to drive you in style to the jet."

"No bullets? But how—"

"Ten minutes." He was gone, striding through the crowd in the direction of the departure gate.

She gazed after him in exasperation and bewilderment. Just how did he think he could dispose of two soldiers with machine guns when it was obvious he wasn't even armed?

Still, there was a cool confidence that reflected both competence and absolute assurance in Nilsen's manner, and heaven only knew when she'd get out of Zarbondal if she didn't take advantage of this opportunity. She wished she weren't so blasted tired. She was certainly in no shape to make an important decision. The frightening events of the last few days that had culminated in her being left alone and vulnerable in this forsaken airport had brought her to the point of emotional exhaustion. She stood, hesitating for a moment, trying to weigh her options. They were pitifully few.

Oh, what the hell? she asked herself.

She whirled on her heel and moved swiftly toward the bank of lockers against the far wall.

The baggage truck pulled up in front of the departure door. Gunner Nilsen jumped out, threw her suitcases into the bed of the truck, and easily lifted her into the seat beside his. "I do like a punctual woman." He gave her a roguish wink before running around the snubnosed front of the vehicle and climbing into the driver's seat. "Particularly in circumstances like this. The machine gun is out of commission, but the men in the tower just might call for reenforcements. I want to be out of Zarbondal before that happens."

He drove the truck across the field, cutting blithely across taxi lanes and runways toward the north-south runway where the Learjet had previously landed. He gave a mocking salute as he passed the tower. "Adieu and good riddance."

"How did you get rid of the machine guns?" Quenby cautiously looked over her shoulder at the roof of the terminal building. There was no one in view.

"They were amateurs." He shrugged. "But then, revolutionaries usually are amateurs who neglect seeking support from powerful segments of the population. That's why so few revolutions succeed."

She shot him a curious glance. "You seem to have made a study of the subject."

"I became interested a few years ago, when I followed the revolution in Tamrovia. I started reading everything I could get my hands on about the history and the dynamics of revolution." He made a face. "Jon, Andrew's father, thought I was planning on starting another Bolshevik uprising. I don't have the reputation for being so dedicated in my scholastic endeavors. I like my acquisition of knowledge to be both painless and desultory." He parked the vehicle, his gaze on the northern horizon. He checked his watch. "One more minute."

"You expect your pilot to be on the dot?"

He looked at her in surprise. "Of course. Marta's always on time. She wouldn't be permitted to fly a Clanad plane if she weren't superbly qualified and absolutely reliable."

"Clanad? Is that the name of a corporation?"

Quenby asked, puzzled. "According to the information I received from my agency, my job was to be nanny to the child of an executive of Sedikhan Oil, a friend of Sheikh Alex Ben Raschid."

"Well, it's sort of a corporation, and Jon and Alex *are* very good friends."

"But the sheikh isn't Jon Sandell's employer?"

"In a way," Gunner Nilsen said vaguely. "I don't know exactly how it works. I think the Clanad develops and Alex arranges distribution."

Quenby gazed at him in frustration. 'Sort of a corporation?' She knew even less now than she had before. "And what do you do in this organization, Mr. Nilsen?"

"Gunner." He turned to her and smiled with heart-stopping warmth. "I guess you'd say I'm kind of a troubleshooter for the Clanad. I straighten out the problems that crop up occasionally."

"Like those men with the machine guns?" she asked clearly. "Just what kind of an organization is this Clanad?"

"I told you—" He broke off as he comprehended her meaning. "You think we're something like the Mafia?" He suddenly threw back his head and began to laugh. "No way. We're depressingly law-abiding these days."

"These days? I take it you weren't in the past?"

His smile faded. "We had a few problems to iron out before we were able to reach a compromise with society." His gaze searched her face. "Would it make a difference to you if Andrew's father were a criminal?"

Would it? Quenby wasn't sure. She didn't want

to become involved with gangsters or even with someone skirting dangerously close to the edge of the law. Yet the agency had said the child Andrew had a very special problem and children weren't responsible for the sins of their parents. "I'm not sure," she said. "I'd have to meet Andrew first."

Smiling, Gunner shook his head. "You're a goner."

"I beg your pardon?"

"We've got you," he said with satisfaction. "You're soft as marshmallow beneath all that crisp practicality. One look at Andrew and you're going to go into a tailspin."

"I am *not* soft. Naturally I have a certain fondness for children or I wouldn't be in this profession, but I'm hardly a pushover."

He smiled, his expression gentle. "Hey, it's all right to be soft. I like it. I'm squishy as a summer snowball myself where kids are concerned."

"But not when soldiers with machine guns are on the scene?"

"Nope." He abruptly stood up and waved his arm in a wild arc at the jet that was now approaching the runway. "There's Marta now. I told her not to come in if we weren't waiting here on the runway."

The Learjet landed like a feather. Marta was evidently as good a pilot as Gunner had claimed, Quenby thought admiringly as the plane taxied toward them. "What would she have done if we hadn't been here?"

"Taken Andrew back to Sedikhan."

"And left you here?" she asked, surprised.

"I told you we don't take chances with Andrew's life." He glanced at the tower. "Our friends seem a little too quiet. Let's get the hell out of here."

The door of the Learjet was opened by a pleasant-faced woman in her late fifties whose petite body appeared splendidly fit. Her sleek short gray hair shone with vitality and contrasted beautifully with the trim scarlet jump suit she was wearing. She let down a ladder, and Gunner passed Quenby's suitcases up to her. "Any trouble?" she asked as the couple climbed the stairs.

"Not much," Gunner said. "Marta Danbrow this is Quenby Swensen."

"How do you do?" Quenby murmured. "And I'm afraid I don't have the necessary stiff upper lip to regard guerrillas with machine guns as 'not much.' "

"Gunner's accustomed to a certain amount of hassle," Marta said. "I think he cut his teeth on a bazooka." Her handshake was as firm and pleasant as her face. "Make yourself comfortable." She nodded at a curtained alcove in the back of the plane. "Andrew is napping right now, but he should be awake in about"—she glanced inquiringly at Gunner—"forty minutes, Gunner?"

"Fifty five," he said. "I allowed a little extra time for emergencies."

The precision of the statement could mean only one thing, and Quenby's blue-green eyes were suddenly blazing. "You gave that child a sedative to keep him out of the way?"

"I didn't say—"

"Dammit, what else could it be?" Her hands

clenched into fists at her sides. "Andrew is in my charge now, and I do not approve of using drugs on children except in the most extreme circumstances. I won't have a child in—"

"Hold it." Gunner held up his hand to silence her. "Easy. No drugs. I promise you, Quenby."

"Then what?"

"Hypnosis," he said. "Andrew is an excellent subject; he's been trained since he was an infant to respond. Jon and Elizabeth agree with you about the use of drugs and think it's much healthier in the case of illness to have Andrew able to avoid sedatives as much as possible."

"Andrew is crazy about Gunner," Marta added. "He's an extremely sensitive child, and when we realized what the situation was on the ground, we were afraid Andrew would become too upset if he knew Gunner might be in danger."

"I see." Quenby's expression was still troubled. "I don't know much about hypnosis."

"It's harmless," Gunner said gently. "I love Andrew. I'd never do anything that wasn't in his best interest. Do you believe me, Quenby?"

She couldn't help but believe him. His gaze holding her own was direct and absolutely without guile. "I believe you."

"Good. Now sit down and buckle up. I'm going up to the cockpit with Marta and try to persuade her to let me fly the plane." He smiled coaxingly at the pilot. "You did promise that if I were very good, you'd let me at those controls."

"When have you ever been even marginally good?" Marta asked as she strode toward the cockpit. "Do you call risking your neck proper behavior, for heaven's sake? What do you think the committee would say if they knew you'd taken such a chance as you just did?"

"Good riddance to bad rubbish?" Gunner asked flippantly as he trailed behind her.

"You know better than that." She gave him a stern glance over her shoulder. "You're so valuable to all of us, Gunner. You have no right to be reckless with—"

The rest of her words were lost to Quenby as the door to the cockpit closed behind them.

She gazed at the door blankly for a long moment, feeling as if she had been picked up and tossed into the middle of a hurricane. Good Lord, what was she getting herself into?

Gunner Nilsen was the most extraordinary man she had ever met. His charm was mesmerizing. Why else was she on this plane when she wasn't at all sure she wasn't actually becoming involved with a criminal group? Still, if Gunner were a gangster, he certainly wasn't the stereotyped villain, and Marta Danbrow appeared to be as wholesome as her own grandmother Ingrid.

The plane began to taxi down the runway, and Quenby hurriedly crossed to the plush wine-colored chair Marta had indicated, sat down, and fastened her seat belt. She leaned back, closing her eyes and trying to relax. After all, she was not committing herself by accepting a plane trip back to the U.S. She would make her own decision based on cool reason when the time came.

Gunner Nilsen probably wouldn't waste his

charm trying to sway her to his way of thinking. Men of his attractiveness had women battling for every smile, and seldom devoted much attention to the Quenby Swensens of this world.

Yes, when the time came, she would make a decision that had nothing to do with Gunner Nilsen.

"Coffee?"

Quenby opened her eyes to see Marta Danbrow standing beside her extending a cup from which a fragrant vapor was rising. "Yes, thank you." Quenby took the cup and sipped the steaming black beverage gingerly. It tasted exotically of cinnamon and ginger. She looked at Marta in surprise. "It's quite good, but I've never tasted anything exactly like it."

"Gunner likes his coffee this way. He acquired a taste for it in Sedikhan." Marta made a face. "I prefer it plain myself, but the catering staff at the Marasef airport is principally female and I believe they spend half their time trying to figure out what Gunner wants, and the other half trying to make sure he gets it." She smiled at Quenby. "I guess I should have become accustomed to it over the years."

"You've worked with him before?"

"I've been his pilot for four years. Gunner's qualified to fly himself, but the Clanad was afraid he'd be too reckless and assigned me to him. They thought my gray hair and advanced years might have a calming influence on him." She shook her head. "Scratch that. The first thing Gunner did was buy me several of these flashy red jump suits, the second was tell me no one with any sense would consider an attractive lady like me as calming old grandmother material. Then he proceeded to fix me up with a couple of his more mature friends." She shrugged helplessly. "Before I knew it, he had me exactly where he wanted me."

Quenby looked down into the depths of her coffee cup. "And where was that?"

Marta grimaced. "I alternate being under his thumb and wrapped around his little finger."

Quenby could not imagine this brusque, assertive lady being in either position. "He sounds manipulative."

"Gunner?" Marta shook her head. "Manipulative is too cold a word. He does change his surroundings to suit himself, but he never tries to use people. And, somehow, everything seems a little better for his interference." Her face softened. "Gunner is quite a man."

And Marta Danbrow was obviously as thoroughly under his spell as she had claimed, Quenby thought. "Did you let him take off?"

Marta nodded as she straightened and stood up. "He knew I would. Gunner can read people damn well without going underneath. He has an instinct—"

Underneath? Quenby was about to question that curious phrasing, when Marta turned away. "I'd better get back to the cockpit before Gunner decides to take us to the Bahamas instead of Albany. He's fully capable of doing that, you know."

"I'm afraid I don't know. He's a stranger to me."

Marta's glance was shrewd as she looked over her shoulder. "And you don't trust him?"

Quenby's gaze met Marta's. "Should I? You've just told me he's both reckless and spoiled."

"The first is true, but I never said he was spoiled. Gunner may get everything he wants, but it's not because he demands it. It's because he's"—she hesitated, thinking about it—"loving."

"Loving?"

She nodded. "I guess I never analyzed it before. It's natural to want to give to someone who loves you and thinks you're special. Well, Gunner thinks everyone is special and I truly believe there aren't many people he doesn't love."

"You're painting me a very strange picture of a troubleshooter."

"You'll see." Marta reached for the handle of the door to the cockpit. "And I never said he wasn't unusual."

The entire setup was unusual, Quenby thought in bewilderment. A corporation that assigned grandmothers to troubleshooters to keep them from being too reckless, a child who had a mysterious problem, a man who gained adulation because he was "loving."

If she were smart, she would board the first flight to Minnesota when the Learjet touched down in Albany. It had been a long time since she had been back to the farm for a visit with her family.

She had enough money saved to last for a few months. It wasn't as if she had to take this job.

Gunner Nilsen opened the door of the cockpit, calling back over his shoulder, "But Monte Carlo is so pretty in May. What difference would one day make?"

"Albany," Marta said sternly.

Gunner sighed. "Oh, all right. I just thought Quenby would like some R and R." He closed the door and strolled toward her, an amiable smile on his face. "Well, I tried. Marta can be as tough as a top sergeant I had when I was in the army." He dropped into the seat next to her and she became aware of the clean scent of soap and a spicy aftershave. "It looks as if we're going straight to New York State. Pity. I really would have liked to have seen you in an emerald Dior gown, tossing chips onto a roulette table." His gaze narrowed thoughtfully on her face. "Maybe with a cigarette in a long jade holder."

"I don't gamble, I'm not likely to ever own a Dior gown, and I don't smoke," she said crisply. "Monte Carlo would be wasted on me. You've got the wrong woman."

A slow smile lit his face. "I don't think so. I've got an idea I definitely have the right woman. Now all I have to do is to get you used to the idea."

She experienced again that peculiar breathlessness, and she hastily took another sip of coffee. "I'm sure you're accustomed to glamorous women who fit into that Monte Carlo scene, but I assure you I'd be out of place. I don't have a jet-set mentality."

"I know." He grinned. "That's why you'd be so wonderful there. It would be a great game for you. You wouldn't take all that nonsense seriously, you'd just enjoy it."

After thinking about it, Quenby realized in surprise that she probably would enjoy herself as much as he had said she would. "You're very perceptive."

"About some things. I have a blind spot or two, but I guess it's natural that I be attuned to you." He was gazing at her intently. "I'm glad you don't smoke."

"Why?"

"I'd worry about you," he said simply.

Golden warmth spread through her like waves of sunshine. She pulled her gaze away from him with an effort. "It's only sensible not to smoke when it might endanger my health."

"But I've already told you that I don't believe you're always guided by your head."

"I said you were perceptive, not a mind reader," Quenby said. "You don't know me well enough to make those kinds of judgments."

A faint smile tugged at his lips. "I wouldn't presume to suggest I'd read your mind." His smile faded. "But I feel I know quite a bit about you, Quenby. You were thoroughly investigated before you were even considered for the job."

Her gaze flew to his face. "Investigated?"

"Don't be so indignant. You can understand that Jon and Elizabeth had to know Andrew would be safe with you."

"My employment agency in London has a complete dossier on me. I don't see why any further investigation was required."

"The dossier told us only the surface information," Gunner said, looking at the ceiling of the cabin. "Quenby Swensen, twenty-seven years old, unmarried, born and raised on a dairy farm two hundred miles from St. Paul, Minnesota, the oldest child in a family of four brothers and three sisters. Attended a university in Minneapolis as a music major, studying the harp." He gazed directly into her eyes now. "We don't know why you decided to quit music when you were recruited by a prestigious school in London that trains and places nannies with people around the world. You spent eighteen months studying there, and you've had three assignments since your graduation. You were nanny to the hyperactive daughter of a film star, then to the asthmatic child of a French automobile manufacturer, and finally to the prime minister's handicapped son. Your employers all praised you to the skies and offered you very generous amounts of money to stay." He paused. "But you refused. The longest you consented to stay with any child was two years. Your Mrs. Dalkeith at the agency assumed you liked a challenge and that once the child's problem was on the way to being solved, you lost interest. We thought so, too, until we received the report from our own people."

"Really?" Her tone was guarded. "And what did they find out to change your mind?"

"That you were afraid to stay," he said gently. "You have very strong emotions and you became attached to those children. It was probably terribly wrenching leaving each position as it was. You couldn't afford to stay longer and risk becoming completely involved with a child that wasn't your own."

Shock rippled through her. She felt suddenly naked and exposed. "Your psychological profile must have been considerably in depth."

His hand suddenly covered hers on the arm of the seat. "Don't freeze up on me. I can feel you—" He stopped. "Listen, it's beautiful to be able to care as much as you do. There are so few people who can love with their whole heart and soul. Most of us tend to divide ourselves up into compartments so that we don't give too much, but you don't do that. You give everything and hold back nothing. That's a rare gift, Quenby."

Her hand was tingling beneath his strong, vital clasp. She should move it away. His touch was causing a stirring deep within her and she knew exactly what that stirring meant. She didn't want to feel sexually aroused by this golden-haired rogue. He was everything that was exotic and they had absolutely nothing in common. She would be idiotic to read anything into a few cryptic sentences from a man who was obviously accustomed to getting whatever he wanted from women.

She moistened her lips with her tongue. "I'm not ashamed of having an affectionate nature. I merely choose not to put it on display for all and sundry."

"But I'm not all and sundry." His hand tightened. "I'm Gunner and you're safe with me. I'll never hurt you as LaCroix did."

"LaCroix!" Her eyes widened. "Your report *was* very thorough." She jerked her hand away. "And intrusive. My personal life is my own, dammit. It has nothing to do with my qualifications for any employment."

He grimaced. "Sorry. That slipped out. You're right, that report places me in an unfair position. Would you like to hear about Mary Ann?"

She gazed at him in bewilderment. "Mary Ann?"

"Mary Ann Minot, she was my last affair. I'm sure she wouldn't mind me telling you about her. Nice woman, we had a great time together. Nothing serious like your relationship with Raoul LaCroix." He frowned. "I don't think I like the idea of the two of you together. I never thought I was the jealous type but—"

"What on earth are you talking about?"

He looked at her in surprise. "I'm trading my affair for yours. That way we start out even."

"We're not starting out at all. We're strangers."

He nodded cheerfully. "Isn't that great? I've been tempted to sneak a peek ever since I saw you, but I decided I don't want to know everything at once. I want to save you and watch you unfold bit by bit."

Sneak a peek? The man was totally bewildering.

"Besides, it's more fair to you that I wait. I don't want to take advantage of you." He suddenly chuckled. "Well, I do, but not that way."

She gazed at him in helpless fascination. "In what way then?"

"Oh, hell, I was going to try to be discreet. I should have known I'd never make it. I guess I might as well be frank with you." A reckless smile touched his lips. "I intend to play your lovely body like the strings of a harp and then I'm going to learn every single melody that you've stored up inside you and teach you every one that makes me what I am." He paused. "And if we're lucky, we'll continue to make music together for the next fifty years or so."

He couldn't be serious. "How poetic." She smiled with an effort. "It's a good thing we've established how sensible I am or I might think you meant it. Do you always make passes at your godchild's nannies?"

"You're the first one he's had." His lips twisted in a lopsided smile. "You don't believe in me?"

"Of course not. I'm hardly the type of woman a man instantly loses his head over." She carefully kept her tone cool and objective. "I'm fairly intelligent and reasonably attractive, but I'm definitely not a femme fatale. Nor would I want to be. I've always thought the Delilahs of this world must be very uncomfortable. I definitely prefer to be merely in the average category."

Average? His gaze moved over her shining shoulder-length hair that was a shade somewhere between ash and pale gold, and then to the fine contours of her face. She actually believed her assessment of her physical appearance, Gunner thought incredulously. What kind of idiot had LaCroix been to make her doubt how special and

lovely she was? Then he felt a jolt of fierce pleasure surge through him. He was going to be the
one who showed her what she was and could be.
How lucky could a man be?

But not now. He had already gone too fast and
too far today. She was beginning to be uneasy
and soon would be backing away from him. "I've
always liked tall Scandinavian blondes," he said
with deliberate lightness. "It's a terrible weakness.
You're of Swedish descent, aren't you?"

"Yes." He had been merely amusing himself just
as she had thought. Quenby ignored the odd pang
the realization brought. "My grandparents Ingrid
and Olaf came to Minnesota in 1915, when they
were in their teens. Nilsen is a Swedish name too,
isn't it?"

"Yes, but I can't claim a Swedish heritage.
Nilsen's not my real name. Jon thought I looked
Swedish, and when I needed to switch to an alias
I chose Nilsen."

"Alias?" she repeated warily. "Why should you
need an alias?"

"Ah, suspicion rears its ugly head again." He
studied her. "I'd like to be honest with you, but I
think it will be easier if I unfold for you bit by bit
too."

"I don't know if I want to risk going into any
position blindfolded."

"But you will." His smile lit his deeply tanned
face with glowing warmth. "Because I've got an
ace in the hole. You haven't met Andrew. One
look and you'll be a goner."

"You said that before," she said impatiently. "My judgment won't be clouded by—"

"Is it all right if I get up now?"

They both turned toward the curtained alcove at the rear of the compartment. That endearingly hoarse, gravelly voice had come from the throat of a little boy whose small, solid frame was garbed in tennis shoes, blue jeans, and a yellow *Star Trek* T-shirt.

Quenby sighed with resignation as she realized Gunner was correct. If this was Andrew, she was, indeed, a goner.

Two

"Sure," Gunner said, and held out his hand. "We've been waiting for you to wake up, haven't we, Quenby? Come over here and I'll introduce you to the lady."

Andrew flew across the compartment to Gunner, nestling in the curve of his arm with affection and perfect trust. "I know who she is. How do you do," he said gravely, holding out his hand with touching dignity. "I've been looking forward to meeting you, Miss Swensen."

Quenby wanted to reach out and hug him. Sparkling brown eyes gazed into her own with the fearless goodwill of a child who had known only love and trust. The child's silky skin and tousled golden hair contrasted oddly with that gravelly voice, but the combination was so warm and sunny it would have melted an iceberg.

Careful to show no hint of condescension, Quenby shook Andrew's hand. "And I've been looking forward to meeting you too, Andrew. Did you have a nice nap?"

The faintest shadow flickered over the child's face and then was gone as he cuddled even closer to Gunner. "It wasn't . . . bad."

Gunner's arm tightened around Andrew's shoulders for the briefest instant. "Dreams?"

Andrew didn't answer for a moment. "Shadows . . ." He suddenly smiled, and Quenby caught her breath. Radiance, sweetness, mischief. "Next time I want to go with you. You have all the fun, Gunner. What happened?"

"Nothing much. I just waltzed in and picked up Quenby and her luggage and waltzed right out again."

Andrew shook his head skeptically. "You wouldn't have put me to sleep if you hadn't expected trouble. Next time you have to take me along."

Gunner laughed. "The very next time that Quenby is in trouble I'll let *you* waltz in and get her. Okay?"

Andrew turned to Quenby, a hint of mischief in his eyes. "Are you expecting any trouble soon?"

Quenby burst out laughing. "I don't see anything on the immediate horizon, but I'll be sure to let you know if anything crops up."

"Thank you." He inclined his head in a quaint bow of acknowledgment that was delightfully old-world. "But don't tell Gunner, he's very selfish about hogging all the adventures for himself."

"I'll remember," Quenby said solemnly.

"May I go up front with Marta?" Andrew turned to Gunner with scarcely contained eagerness. "She's teaching me to work the radio."

Gunner nodded. "But tell her to give you a glass of orange juice before you get down to the basics."

Andrew made a face. "I don't like orange juice. I'd rather have some of your coffee."

"Too much caffeine. Besides, I'm very selfish about hogging that too."

An uneasy frown wrinkled Andrew's brow. "I was joking, you know. I didn't really mean you were selfish. You're not— "

Gunner reached out and gently touched Andrew's lips with two fingers, silencing him. "I knew you were joking." His gaze was suddenly intent on the child's face. "You should have realized that, Andrew. If you had let yourself, you would have known—"

Andrew hurriedly stepped back. "I'll drink the orange juice." He smiled at Quenby. "See you later." Then he was running toward the door of the cockpit.

Quenby's gaze followed Andrew until the door closed behind him. "He's adorable," she said. "I think I'm in love."

"It's a common affliction," Gunner said. "We're all crazy about Andrew."

"He seems much older than five. He expresses himself beautifully."

Gunner's gaze went to the door of the cockpit. "He could express himself a hell of a lot better."

"I don't agree. He appears very bright."

His gaze returned to her face. "He has an extraordinarily high IQ. It's best that you realize that at once. Andrew cut his teeth on Einstein and you can't treat him as you would an ordinary child." His intent expression softened. "Though sometimes he acts as nutty as any other kid."

"Is that Andrew's problem? Gifted children often have trouble adjusting to society."

"Only partially," Gunner said. "Actually, his problem is much more complex."

Quenby waited, but he failed to elaborate. "Well, how can I help him if you don't tell me what the difficulty is?" she finally asked in exasperation.

"You'll help him by being Quenby Swensen." His index finger reached out to touch her cheek. "I've set up a situation that I hope will force him to correct his problem himself."

"And what part do I play in this situation?"

"Nothing very strenuous. I've rigged another catalyst and yours is only a passive role. You're to surround Andrew with love and support when he needs it. You'll be the nice billowy cushion he falls back on when the going gets tough. Elizabeth, his mother, would have come, but they're too close. We believed Andrew was more likely to take independent action if she weren't there to lean on."

"But you want me to support him," she said tartly. "You're not making any sense."

"I know." He smiled. "Sorry. All the pieces will fit together eventually. I promise you I'll tell you everything as soon as I think you're ready to accept it."

"Accept *what*, for heaven's sake?"

His hand fell away from her cheek. "Why did you choose the harp?"

She blinked, bewildered by the abrupt change of subject. "What?"

"The harp is a rather outdated musical instrument and it's not exactly portable. Why a harp?"

"I fell in love with it when I saw Harpo Marx play one on the late, late movie. I thought I'd never heard anything so beautiful and—" She stopped. "You don't have to throw out red herrings to get me off the subject. I much prefer frankness. If you don't want to discuss something, just say so."

Gunner grinned. "I didn't want to discuss my plans, but I also wanted to know why you chose the harp. I want to know everything about you." His smile faded, his gaze narrowed on her face. "Every single thing."

Quenby felt the color rush to her cheeks and knew, with her damnably fair skin, he would notice she was blushing. She hurriedly looked away. "I won't be a party to anything illegal. My duties will only concern the care of Andrew."

"Right." Gunner nodded solemnly. "When I meet with the members of the Mafia and Cosa Nostra, I'll make sure I don't do it on the premises."

"And I'd appreciate it if you'd keep our relationship on a strictly business basis and refrain from trying to—" She hesitated.

"Seduce you?" Gunner suggested. "No deal. Except it won't be seduction. I'll just be leading you to accept what we both know is right for us." He met her gaze. "If that's a qualification, I'll have to find another cushion for Andrew and continue our relation on another level."

"But can't you see . . ." She trailed off in defeat. His expression showed that he was absolutely determined. "You're very big on my accepting everything with no proof whatever. What about you?"

"I have a few things to accept as well. This is all new to me. I'm used to skating on the surface and suddenly I'm floundering over my head." His expression became oddly stern. "But I *will* accept it, Quenby. Because I believe we all have to accept what we are and then try to reach out to be something better. And we can be better . . . together."

She was utterly baffled. "Gunner, I don't—"

"Hush." His fingers silenced her as they had Andrew only a few moments before. "I'll go slow. I'm not good at being patient, but I can learn. I'm very good at learning new things." His hand left her lips and once more enveloped her own. He leaned back in his chair. "Now, shall I tell you about Mill Cottage?"

He felt the tension begin to ebb from her. "Mill Cottage?"

"That's where we'll be spending the summer. It's Andrew's mother's family home and over two hundred years old. It's located on a stream and used to be a flour mill and has a genuine paddle wheel that still works."

"It sounds charming."

"Oh, it is. Elizabeth loves Mill Cottage and she wanted Andrew to see it. Most of the furniture is antique but comfortable, and the house is out in the country just north of Albany. There are woods and meadows nearby." He continued to describe Mill Cottage and the surrounding countryside. With every word he could feel the tautness leaving Quenby's rigid muscles. She was so tense. That bastard LaCroix must have really done a number on her to make her this wary. He felt a sudden surge of savage anger explode inside him. Shock rippled through him. Damn, he had thought he'd gotten it under control. He hadn't felt this white-hot rage since the night he had come home to find his mother and father lying— He blocked the thought quickly. He knew pain and anger accomplished nothing and was a danger to someone of his temperament. He *knew* that. He had to bury the thought of that night.

"Gunner, are you all right?" Quenby was looking worriedly at him.

He smiled a careless smile. "I guess I was daydreaming. Where was I? Oh, yes, Mill Cottage. I've hired a full-time handyman, and a maid to come in twice a week. I'll do the cooking if you don't mind. I like it."

"No, I don't mind." She settled back on the cushioned softness of the seat.

He hadn't been daydreaming. It was too soft a word for the thoughts that had turned Gunner Nilsen's face into a flinty mask of hate. She shivered suddenly as she recalled the word that had occurred to her in that fleeting moment before he had returned from the dark world of his thoughts and become again the debonair, golden man she had assumed was Gunner Nilsen. The word that was as ancient and mystical as its Nordic concept, as frightening as it was fierce.

Berserker.

The man standing before the front door of Mill Cottage was dressed in rough sunfaded jeans and a blue chambray work shirt. He shifted restlessly, every muscle of his huge, big-boned frame alive with eagerness. He rushed to the car, opening the driver's door almost before the car had pulled to a stop. "Hello there, Mr. Nilsen. I did it. I scrubbed the floors and I built the platform. I fixed the swing and I mowed the lawn." His hazel eyes were shining. "I did it all just like you said."

"That's good, Steven." Gunner's voice was gentle as he got out of the driver's seat and came around to open the passenger door for Quenby. "I'm sure you did a great job too." He helped Quenby from the car and then opened the rear door for Andrew. "Quenby, this is Steven Blount. He's going to help us out this summer."

He was a child, Quenby thought with a wrenching pang of sympathy. Steven looked to be in his early forties, his dark hair just beginning to be flecked with gray, his craggy face seamed by time and sun, but his eyes still held the clear wonder of a little child. "I'm very glad to meet you, Steven."

He nodded. "Me too." His gaze passed over her to Andrew, and he smiled tentatively. "You're Andrew. Mr. Nilsen told me all about you. He said we could play together when I wasn't working. I built you a real good platform for a treehouse. I thought we'd decide how you wanted it before we built the house."

Andrew was looking at him with a strange expression on his face. It was a moment before Quenby could identify it as recognition. "I'd like to see it."

Steven's face lit up. "Right now?"

Andrew looked at Gunner. "May I?"

Gunner nodded. "Run along. I wouldn't want to be the one to impede architectural progress. Dinner will be ready in about an hour and a half."

Steven hurried around the car to stand beside Andrew. "You're going to like it. It's in a maple tree in those woods across the stream. If we lay down on the platform and stay real quiet, the squirrels will come up and play all around us. Sometimes they let me touch them."

"I know I'll like it." Andrew's voice was soft as he gazed at Steven. "I don't know much about squirrels, but we have peacocks in the garden at home in Marasef. I'll tell you about them." He slipped his small hand into the man's big, callused one with an odd air of protectiveness. "Show me."

Quenby watched them walk away, and for some reason she felt her throat tighten helplessly. The small child, the huge man, both caught in this golden hour of childhood. But time would soon carry Andrew beyond this hour, while the man would remain there forever.

"You don't have to worry about Andrew," he said. Gunner's gaze was on her face. "Steven is very gentle. When I first met him, he reminded me of Andrew. They both shine inside."

"Shine?"

"Haven't you noticed how some people give off a kind of radiance? Steven is beautiful inside. He'd never let Andrew be hurt."

"I know that." Quenby's gaze returned to the handyman and Andrew now crossing the small arched wooden bridge over the stream. "But somehow I think it will be Andrew who'll be the caretaker."

Gunner nodded. "Andrew is very protective of those he cares about."

Quenby's gaze shifted to his face. "And you knew he'd care about Steven, didn't you?"

"I hoped he would. The odds were in my favor. If I could see Andrew in Steven, then I thought Andrew also would be able to see Steven as a soulmate."

"Is Steven actually retarded?"

"There's no physical damage that could cause retardation, he just has an extremely low IQ. He was in a home for the insane until he was thirty-two. His mother abandoned him when he was five and, when he proved inadequate to cope in the orphanage, they sent him to the state institution. It was only recently the state investigated and found several of the inmates to be perfectly sane."

"How tragic," Quenby said huskily. "What a terrible waste."

"Since then Steven's been washing dishes and doing odd jobs around the sanitorium. It was the only home he knew and he was a little lost on the outside."

"I can see how he would be." Steven and Andrew were in the thick stand of maple trees across the meadow and almost out of sight as Quenby turned toward the front door. "Which room shall we give Andrew? It seems he hasn't much interest in anything as mundane as this house."

"The room at the head of the stairs. It's Elizabeth's old room and overlooks the paddle wheel. She said she wanted to think of him there in the place where she grew up." Gunner strode around the car and unlocked the trunk. "Go on inside and look around. I'll bring in the suitcases and take them upstairs. You might put on a pot of coffee."

"I don't know how to make that exotic mixture you call coffee."

"I'll settle for the plain American variety." He opened the trunk and began to take out the suitcases and set them on the gravel driveway. "I'll teach you how to make real coffee tomorrow."

"I don't believe that was in my job description," she said dryly. "But I'll consider it."

"You'll need something to keep you busy if Andrew and Steven get along as well as I think they will. You can't play the harp all the time."

"If you have Steven, why do you need me?" she asked in exasperation. "It's obvious you believe I won't be earning my salary."

"You'll be earning it." Gunner slammed the trunk shut. "When he needs you, you'll be there. A nice soft—" He broke off, his head lifting like that of a forest animal scenting danger, his light eyes suddenly alert and wary. His gaze slowly shifted to

the thick foliage of the woods across the road
from the house.

"Is there something wrong?" Quenby's gaze followed Gunner's to the woods. There was nothing
unusual, no sound, not even a breath of wind
stirring the trees.

"Probably not. I thought for a moment . . ." He
shrugged. "Go inside. I'll be right in."

Quenby started up the steps toward the Dutch
door. The ivy-covered stone cottage was really lovely,
she thought, it was no wonder Andrew's mother
was so fond of Mill Cottage. "Is the kitchen stocked
with groceries? If I'm to make coffee, I'll need . . ."
The words trailed off as she glanced over her shoulder. Gunner was still staring at the woods across
the road, and the expression on his face was as
hard and savage as the one he had worn for that
brief instant on the plane. "Gunner?"

His glance immediately met her own, and he
smiled reassuringly. "Sorry. This place brings back
memories, some of them not very pleasant." He
picked up two of the suitcases. "I had the cleaning
woman go shopping for us and stock the refriger-
ator. The coffee should be in one of the cabinets.
Give me twenty minutes, will you? I need time to call
Sedikhan and tell Jon and Elizabeth we've arrived
safely."

Quenby nodded. "Twenty minutes." She opened
the door and disappeared into the house.

"Put Jon on the phone, will you, Elizabeth?"
Gunner deliberately kept his tone light. "Now that

you know your pride and joy is well and flourishing, I need to know whether to keep the Learjet here or send it back to Sedikhan. I'll be sure to have Andrew call you before he goes to bed tonight."

It was only a moment before Jon came on the line. "What's this about the jet? I thought we'd agree you'd send it back. You won't need Marta or—"

"There may be something wrong, Jon," Gunner cut in crisply. "I didn't want to worry Elizabeth. Is she still in the room?"

"Yes."

"Then I'll try to pose my questions for a yes or no answer. Our report was that Karl Bardot had disappeared from view after he was discredited and discharged from the NIB. Have there been any reports of his surfacing since then?"

There was a pause on the other end of the line as the implication of the question sank home. "No," Jon said. "None."

"And the organization has definitely been disbanded?"

"No question about it. We investigated very thoroughly before we took the chance of—" Jon broke off. "You don't agree?"

"I don't know about the NIB, but Karl Bardot may be very much on the scene." Gunner's hand tightened on the receiver. "And damn close."

"Why?"

"I *felt* him, dammit. You don't forget touching someone with that ugliness inside him. You know that, Jon."

"Yes, I know that," Jon said heavily. "You're sure?"

"Hell, I don't know. It was only for a split-second and it could have been my mind playing tricks on me. I have very strong memories of this place and Bardot." He drew a deep breath. "Do you want me to abort?"

"It's your decision."

"It's all going so well," Gunner said with frustration. "Andrew's reaction was just what we thought it would be. I'd stake anything it's going to work, Jon."

"I think you've already made up your mind." Jon's voice took on a steely edge. "Your decision had better be the right one."

"Or you'll cut my throat? You wouldn't have to bother, I'd do it myself. Don't worry, I'll keep Andrew safe. The minute there's anything more concrete to go on, I'll pull him out of here and send him home."

"You bet you will."

"I'll call you tomorrow evening. I could use a man to keep an eye on Andrew and Steven while they're in the woods. Maybe Judd Walker. I've worked with him before."

"He'll be there by tomorrow night."

"Good." Gunner hesitated. "I could be wrong, Jon."

"I've known you for a number of years and your instincts are usually infallible. Rely on them. It's safer."

"Good-bye, Jon."

Gunner replaced the receiver and stood staring

out the bay window in the study. He was scared.
He'd been hoping Jon would lift this responsibility from his shoulders and tell him to come back
to Sedikhan. That moment of recognition had
been so ephemeral that it was entirely possible he
could be wrong, but he didn't *want* to take the
chance of putting Andrew in possible danger. If
these months weren't so vitally important to the
child's health, he'd have bundled everyone into
the car and headed back to the airport.

Because the ugliness that had reached out and
touched him had been as strong as it had been
five years ago, and now he was the only one who
could keep it from hurting Andrew and possibly
even Quenby.

Three

Andrew screamed.

Quenby sat bolt upright in bed. The scream held a wild terror and was followed immediately by sobs.

Quenby swung her feet to the floor, grabbed her robe from the wing chair by the bed, and ran from the room. Seconds later she was throwing open the door to Andrew's room and switching on the overhead light. "Andrew?"

Andrew was sitting up in bed, tears running down his cheeks, eyes wide with terror. His thin shoulders shook with the sobs racking his body.

Quenby flew across the room and enveloped him in her arms. "It's all right. I'm here." Her palm cradled his head as she rocked him back and forth. "You're safe, Andrew. Did you have a bad dream?"

He nodded. His breath came in gasps. "Yes." His arms clung desperately to Quenby. "Shadows . . ."

"It's not surprising you didn't sleep well. This room is strange to you, and you were tired from the trip." Quenby's lips touched his temple. "But it was only a dream, Andrew."

"No, they're waiting." Andrew drew a deep quivering breath and then relaxed against her. "You feel soft, like my mama. Safe."

Quenby felt a warm throb of satisfaction. "Yes, you're safe now." She chuckled suddenly. "And I'm glad you think I'm soft. Do you know what Gunner thinks about when he looks at me? A big fluffy pillow. Isn't that funny?"

The gasps were gradually abating and Andrew lifted his head to look up at her. "Gunner likes you." Tears were hanging from his lashes, and his cheeks were streaked. "He doesn't really think you look like a pillow." He frowned. "Though there was something else about a bed . . ."

Quenby laughed. "What on earth are you talking about? I think you must still be half asleep."

His expression became shuttered. "I'm awake." He drew back out of her arms with an abrupt return to dignity. "I'm sorry I woke you. I'll be fine now."

Quenby wanted to draw him back into her arms and cuddle him, but he was sending out signals that his brief spell of little-boy dependency was over. "Do you have nightmares often?"

He was wiping his eyes on the sleeve of his *Star Trek* pajamas. "Not too often."

Yet he had suffered one only this afternoon, Quenby remembered, and he had murmured that same cryptic word—*shadows*. "Sometimes it helps to talk about a bad dream," she said gently. "It brings it out in the open and into the sunlight. Would you like to tell me about it?"

He shook his head. "It's gone now." He slid down in the bed and drew the sheet up to his chin. "It probably won't come back tonight."

The dream might not come back tonight, but what about other nights? Evidently it was a recurring nightmare. "I'd be glad to listen—if you want to tell me about it."

Andrew closed his eyes. "No, thank you."

The subject was clearly closed. Quenby reached out to stroke his fair hair. "Could I get you something to drink? A cup of hot chocolate?"

"No, thank you."

"A glass of water?"

He shook his head.

Quenby sighed and stood up. Andrew's moment of weakness was behind him and he was once more in control. "Would you like me to sit with you until you get back to sleep?"

He shook his head again.

Quenby hesitated, and then turned toward the door.

"Quenby."

She turned to face him. "Yes?"

His eyes were open again and gazing at her thoughtfully. "Where does Steven sleep?"

"Gunner tells me he has a very nice room and bath over that detached garage."

"As nice as this?" Andrew's gaze traveled around the room, touching on the old rocking chair and the chintz cushions on the window seat. "I like this room. It's kind of . . . warm."

"I don't know if it's quite this nice or not. We could go over there tomorrow and take a look at it if you like."

Andrew nodded seriously. "I think we'd better. Steven needs—" He paused, searching for words. "He's lonely inside. I don't think he's ever had anything that was really his and he needs—" He stopped again. Then he finally shook his head. "I don't know. I'll have to think about it."

"Something warm?" Quenby suggested.

Andrew frowned. "Something . . . beautiful."

Quenby swallowed to ease the sudden tightness of her throat. "Then we'll have to see that he gets what he needs, won't we?"

Andrew nodded, his face lighting with a radiant smile. "Can we give him a birthday party, Quenby? I think he'd like that. He told me that he's never had a birthday present and that he doesn't even know the day he was born. I thought maybe Steven and I could choose a birth date for him and then we could have a party." He shook his head in wonder. "I thought everyone had a birthday."

"Steven hasn't had an easy life, Andrew."

"I know." Andrew was silent for a moment. "It's not fair for some people to have so much and others to have nothing."

"No, it's not fair."

"He won't ever be smart." Andrew's gaze met

Quenby's across the room. "He's not . . . right, is he, Quenby?"

"I believe you should decide that for yourself. I think there are many things that are very right about Steven. He's a kind, gentle man. Gunner says he shines inside."

Andrew nodded. "He does shine. I just wish . . ." He closed his eyes. "It's very puzzling. There should be an answer."

Quenby experienced a poignant pang of sympathy. He was so young to discover that there were some problems that had no answers. "Are you ready to sleep now?"

He nodded. Then his eyes opened once again. "Steven likes stars. He said there was an old man in that place where he lived who knew all about the stars and told Steven all kinds of stories about the constellations. Steven used to lie out in the grass and look up at the stars and think about those stories. He said we could do that in our treehouse. Do we have any books here about stars?"

"I imagine we can find something in the library. It seems to be very well stocked. Can you read, Andrew?"

He looked at her in surprise and indignation. "Of course."

A tiny smile tugged at her lips. "Sorry. I'm not accustomed to five-year-olds who are so advanced. Tomorrow we'll spend a little time in the library before breakfast." She made a face. "Or rather this morning. It's after two o'clock and time for both of us to be asleep." She turned and moved toward the door. "Do you want me to leave the light on?"

"Why?"

She opened the door and turned to look at him. There was genuine surprise on his face. Whatever terror might haunt his dreams, Andrew certainly had no fear of reality. "No reason." She flipped off the overhead light. "Remember, I'm right next door if you need me. Good night, Andrew."

"Good night, Quenby." Andrew's voice was already heavy with drowsiness. "Tomorrow . . ."

Quenby closed the door softly behind her.

"Is something wrong?"

She jumped and then wilted back against the door in relief. Gunner.

"Is Andrew okay?" Gunner was climbing the stairs two at a time and she was surprised to notice he was still fully dressed, even to his black flight jacket.

"You startled me." She took a step forward and put her finger over her lips to caution him to lower his voice. "Nothing's wrong. Andrew had a bad dream but I think he's ready to go back to sleep now."

She couldn't see his expression in the dimness of the hall, but she was aware that some of the tension had left him. "A nightmare?" His voice was low. "Did he tell you about it?"

"No, he didn't tell me about it, though I gathered the dream was one that recurs frequently." She passed him as she started down the stairs. "I want to talk to you."

"Now?"

"Now," she said firmly. "I think it's time we got a few things straight. Come along."

There was a sudden silence before Gunner laughed softly. "Yes, ma'am. Right away, ma'am."

Quenby preceded him down the hall to the big country kitchen at the rear of the house. She switched on the light though there were still embers flickering in the brick fireplace across the room. She sat down at the round oak table and gestured to the chair across the table. "Sit down."

"We could go into the parlor," Gunner suggested. "We'd be more comfortable."

"I don't want to be comfortable. I'm irritated as hell and I want to hold on to that feeling." Quenby drew her loose, flowered cotton robe more closely over her white granny gown. She had forgotten her slippers, she noticed, and the wooden parquet floor was cool beneath her bare feet.

"Would you like me to make coffee?" Gunner asked politely. Then he snapped his fingers. "Sorry. Forget I offered. That would definitely add to your comfort, wouldn't it?" He took off his jacket, draped it over the back of the chair she'd indicated, and sat down across from her. "I gather I'm the one who has aroused your wrath?"

"You're damn right you have. Andrew needs help and you persist in making me work blindfolded." She glared across the table at him. "You knew he wouldn't tell me about his nightmares, didn't you?"

He nodded. "I thought he'd be very hesitant about talking about them."

"And they're part of his problem?"

"More a result than an intrinsic part."

Quenby's lips tightened. "Double-talk."

He leaned back in his chair, studying her. "And you detest any kind of subterfuge, don't you, Quenby? Honesty is very important to you."

"It's important to everyone."

He smiled sadly. "You're wrong, people quite often see only what they want to see. Honesty, like everything else, is how we perceive it."

"Bull," Quenby said clearly. "I'm not sitting here with cold feet in the middle of the night because I want to know your philosophic views. You can be as evasive as you wish about yourself and this mysterious corporation of yours, but Andrew's nightmares concern me. I want to know about them."

"Are your feet cold?" he bent to look under the table. "No wonder. You don't have on any slippers."

"Andrew," Quenby reminded him curtly.

"You have nice feet. Strong . . ." At her exclamation his gaze lifted innocently to her face. "Well, they are. You'd be surprised how few women have nice feet. I bet you went barefoot a lot when you were a kid."

"Of course I went barefoot. I grew up on a farm."

"So did I. There's nothing like feeling the cool grass under your feet, is there? I used to like lying in the meadow and smelling the earth and the grass, feeling the sun on my face."

"You're a farm boy?" Quenby was surprised enough to be distracted momentarily. "You don't

look like someone who'd enjoy the bucolic plea-
sures. I would have pegged you for a cosmopolitan."

"You're right. I couldn't wait to leave the farm
and go out into the real world. We were very poor
and my choices were limited, so I chose the mili-
tary." His expression clouded. "Not a good choice."

"Why not?"

"I found I had a talent for violence. I . . . I liked
it. I had moments when I—" He stopped and was
silent a moment. "Perhaps it's better not to find
out too much about ourselves. If I'd stayed on our
capaza, things would have been very different for
me."

"Better?"

"Who knows? Different anyway." He smiled. "But
then I wouldn't be sitting here with you tonight.
So fate wasn't so unkind after all."

"You believe in fate?"

He looked at her in surprise. "Oh, yes. All Garvanians believe in fate." He shrugged. "However,
we also believe in logic and reason, which makes
us a very confused bunch at times."

"Garvanians," Quenby repeated. She had heard
of Garvania but she couldn't quite recall where or
when. "That's somewhere near Said Ababa, isn't
it?"

"It was." Gunner's smile vanished. "I'm surprised
you even remember it existed. The waters seem to
have closed over it without a ripple. Our kind
neighbor gobbled us up several years ago.
I believe they called the invasion a 'peaceful
annexation.' "

Quenby wanted to reach out and touch him, comfort him. "And it wasn't a 'peaceful annexation'?"

"Bloody. Short but bloody."

"You were a soldier at the time?"

"No, I was detached for a special assignment. I didn't have time to return to my regiment before the war ended." He looked away from her. "Five days. It took only five days for the Said Ababan's to march in, kill and maim and take—" He drew a deep breath, fighting for control. She could see the herculean effort he was expending as he wrestled with memories and emotions too violent for her to imagine. Then his lips curved in a crooked smile. "I'm sorry. This can't be of any interest to you, and I tend to become overly emotional when I think about that period in my life. I'm working on it."

He was sorry. Quenby felt the same surge of maternal tenderness she had experienced when she had comforted Andrew. She had an urge to draw Gunner into her arms and smooth his hair and rock him until the pain went away. Why did he think he had to present an invulnerable mask to hide that pain? "You and Andrew are a great deal alike." She tried to keep all hint of tenderness from her voice. "But I think he may be more sensible."

His hand reached out to cover her own on the table. "I'm sure he is. I've had twenty-five years more to acquire quantities of insecurities and phobias." He turned her hand over and began to rub the inside of her wrist with his thumb. A ripple of heat spread up her arm, and it was suddenly difficult to breathe.

"You're very responsive." His gaze lifted to her face and he smiled with genuine delight. "Your heart just started thumping like crazy. You like me to touch you, don't you?"

"You have a certain amount of sex appeal. You must be aware of that." She tried to withdraw her wrist, but his grasp tightened around it. "Chemistry can occur between a man and woman at very unlikely times. It doesn't mean anything."

"The hell it doesn't," he said softly. "It means I'm getting to you." His thumb resumed its lazy massage of her wrist. "You like my hands on you. That's a big step forward, Quenby. I think you'll like what else I do to you too." He abruptly took her thumb and placed it on his own wrist. "See, you're not alone. My heart is about ready to jump out of my chest, and I'm hurting from wanting you."

She moistened her lips with her tongue. His pulse *was* a strong drumming beneath the pad of her thumb, and the thought that she had caused it was an arousal in itself. "I can't understand why. I don't have on even a smidgin of makeup and my hair is mussed and—"

"And you're not wearing anything beneath that very practical granny gown." The flowered robe had fallen open again and his gaze was fastened on the fullness of her breasts beneath the white cotton of her gown. "I can see the shadows of your nipples beneath the material. You have lovely breasts. Large and well shaped." His gaze lifted with a touch of wistfulness. "I don't suppose you'd let me unbutton your nightgown and look at them?"

"No!" She could barely force the word from her dry throat. She was conscious that her nipples were firming, hardening until they were no longer shadows but boldly prominent. She hurriedly drew her robe more tightly about her.

He made a face. "I didn't think so. Oh, well, I like to look at your face more anyway. Do you realize how pretty you are when the color comes into your cheeks?"

A blush promptly dyed her cheeks scarlet. "That's not kind. I'm so damn fair that I give off signals like a house afire."

"I like it. It's honest, like you. I like everything about you. Your eyes are the exact blue-green of the waters off the coast of Bermuda, and your lower lip has the sweetest curve. Every time I look at it I want to reach out and touch it. I want to touch all of you." His eyes were glowing softly. "Stop fighting, Quenby. Can't you feel how useless it is? This is how we were meant to be. The Clanad's genetics committee claims that attraction is purely scientific, but there's more between us."

"Fate?" Quenby smiled with an effort. "I'm afraid I don't have your Garvanian belief in the power of kismet."

"Because you fell head over heels in love with a louse who used you and then threw you away?

You just got starry-eyed and missed your way. Now you're back on the right track and won't make that mistake again." He grinned. "Destiny Avenue . . . with me waiting at its end. Give me a little time and you won't even remember what that Frenchman looked like."

She was already having trouble remembering Raoul's sleek good looks. His image seemed to be fading, dissolving like a spirit that had been exorcised. He *had* been exorcised, she thought suddenly. She hadn't realized that the pain of his rejection had now healed miraculously after festering for two long years. "I'm not some self-pitying neurotic languishing over a lost love," she said haltingly. "I wouldn't be that stupid."

He nodded as he brought her hand to his lips and kissed the palm lingeringly. "LaCroix wasn't your love. *I'm* your love, and you'll never lose me."

The silence resonated with the simple beauty of his words. "Gunner . . ."

"Will you come to bed with me and let me show you how good we'll be together?" His voice was a level above a whisper. "It will be like nothing either of us have ever felt before. Like walking in a meadow at dawn with the sun on our faces and the whole world just beginning. It will be beautiful, Quenby."

She couldn't seem to tear her gaze away from his eyes. Sun on her face, in her body, a hot blessing of touch and feeling.

He stood up and pulled her to her feet. "Okay?"

She impulsively opened her lips to assent and

then stopped. Crazy. This was crazy. She had just met this man.

Gunner's eyes darkened with disappointment. "No?" He drew a step closer and she became abruptly aware of the heat emanating from his slim, graceful body and the scent of soap and spicy aftershave that clung to him. "You're sure?"

She wasn't sure of anything at the moment. The heat and male fragrance of him was wreathing her in a sensory mist. She realized she was trembling. How idiotic, she was twenty-seven years old, not a schoolgirl. She swallowed. "I think so."

"Why?"

"I don't know you."

Eagerness lit his eyes. "Is that all? Look, I'll let you come in and—" He broke off and his eagerness faded and then died. "I'd probably scare you into a tizzy. *Damn!*"

She was gazing at him in bewilderment.

He shook his head ruefully. "I guess we'll have to go the long way home." He leaned forward and his lips brushed her own with the petal-soft weightlessness of a drifting blossom.

Her lips tingled, throbbed. It seemed impossible that a pressure so ephemeral could leave such aching sensuality in its wake.

"Sweet," he whispered. "Oh, Quenby, wasn't that sweet?"

"Yes." He was still so close that her lips touched his with the word. She had kissed him. Somehow that seemed a momentous happening. She wanted to do it again, to feel that deep tingling on the softness of her lips. Her lips formed the word that was a caress. "Sweet."

His fingers reached up to touch the pulse leaping just beneath her chin. "It's like a hunger. I want more and more." His tongue touched her lower lip. "Open, love, let me in."

Her lips parted and she took his tongue in her mouth. Touching, holding, caressing.

He lifted his head and looked down at her, a deep flush coloring his already tanned cheeks. "It would be like that if you'd let me come into you. Warm . . . tight."

Her breasts were lifting and falling as she tried to force air into her lungs. Dear heaven, if she stayed here one more minute, she would be lost. She took a hasty step back. "I think it's time I went to bed."

He went still. His gaze searched her face and then he said, "You don't mean what I hoped you meant. You come of stronger stock than I do, Quenby love. I'm so hot, I'm about to take off like a rocket." His fingertips brushed her cheek. "All right. We go to our own separate beds . . . for now." He glanced down at her bare feet. "Are they still cold?"

"My feet? I guess so." The words were automatic. She wasn't cold, she was burning. From her cheeks to the arches of her feet. Burning.

"We can't have that." He scooped her up and carried her from the room.

Surprise held her motionless for an instant. "Put me down. I'm too heavy for you to carry."

"You're just right." He strode down the dark

hall and started up the stairs. "Solid enough for me to know I have a woman in my arms."

"A woman who weighs a very solid one hundred thirty pounds and stands five nine in her stocking feet," she said dryly.

"All the better." He didn't seem to be experiencing any difficulty, he wasn't even breathing hard when they reached the top of the stairs.

No, it was she who was breathless, she realized dizzily. "I thought this happened only in the movies."

"What can I say? I like grand gestures. Especially when they mean something." He opened the door of her room and carried her toward the double bed. "And then there's always a chance I'll receive a reward."

"Reward?"

"Nothing much." He set her on her feet beside the bed and slipped the flowered robe off her with the loving matter-of-factness of a mother readying her child for bed. "Hop under the covers. I'll go open the window. It's stuffy in here."

She watched him move toward the window, a dark shadow framed against the moonlight streaming through the panes, before she slipped obediently beneath the covers.

A cool breeze tiptoed through the room trailing the heady fragrance of dew-wet grass and honeysuckle.

"That's better." He turned away from the window and walked toward her. He switched on the lamp on the bedside table and poured her a half glass of water from the carafe beside it. "Drink.

I'm glad you didn't let me make you any coffee. The caffeine would have probably kept you awake." He knelt down beside the bed and handed the glass to her. "Water won't keep you awake but it does help with the dehydration after a plane trip and sometimes fosters a feeling of relaxation."

She gazed bemusedly at the glass in her hand before drinking the water. She handed him back the empty glass. "Thank you. You're being very kind."

His grin was suddenly brimming with mischief. "That's because I want my reward. Sit up, love."

She slowly sat up in bed, a thrill of excitement tingling down her spine. "I thought we'd agreed—"

"I know," he interrupted with a grimace. "And I'm resigned, if not happy. But I do think I deserve something for being so patient." His hands were quickly undoing the four buttons that marched down the front of her granny gown. "It won't hurt you to let me have a peek. I think you'll like it." His hands closed on her breasts still covered by the cotton of her gown.

She gasped as heat cascaded through her. His palms were gentle, but their warmth and strength, their hard maleness, caused a shudder to go through her.

"Your breasts are so heavy." His gaze was intent as he smoothed the thin cotton over her breasts. "Solid and ripe. May I look at you, Quenby?"

She suddenly knew she wanted him to look at her. She nodded, almost breathless with anticipation and excitement.

He gently separated the edges of the material

and then pushed the gown down over her shoulders. It fell to her waist.

Her gaze clung to his face. His expression was taut with tension that was beautifully male and a hunger that reflected the aching emptiness between her own thighs.

He looked at her for a long moment. She could see the pulses pounding in his temples. He slowly reached out and turned off the lamp.

He knelt there in the darkness. She could hear the hoarse sound of his rough breathing. "You want me to put my mouth on you," he said thickly. "You want me to suckle you. You want me to make you swell and firm." He stopped, and his voice rasped with pain as he continued. "I want that too. But it wouldn't stop there."

She waited. Heavy, aching . . . hungry.

"And that would be seduction, wouldn't it, Quenby? I wanted you to come to me without seduction but you told me you weren't ready for me yet." He reached out and carefully drew up the gown over her shoulders and fastened the buttons. "So I'll take the little reward and leave the big one for later." He pushed her down on the pillows and drew the covers up around her throat. His lips feathered her forehead before he stood up. "Good night, Quenby. I'll have breakfast ready by nine in the morning." He moved toward the door, once again a shadow in the moonlit darkness. "Then we'll go for a walk in the woods and watch Steven and Andrew build their treehouse."

"You're not going to tell me about Andrew's

dreams." It was a statement. "I'm still very upset about that, you know."

He opened the door and turned to look at her. "It does you credit." She couldn't see his expression in the dimness but his voice was very gentle. "Soon. There's nothing you could do now even if you did know."

"I like to make decisions of that nature for myself." She suddenly sat up in bed. "I'd better check on Andrew."

"Lie down. I'll do it."

She hesitated and then settled back down on the pillows, a faint smile on her lips. "And will you open his window and give him a drink too?"

"You think that's amusing? I like to do things for people I care about. I find it very satisfying. In every relationship there's usually a caretaker. You recognized that with Steven and Andrew." His voice floated to her in the darkness, soft and fresh as the breeze brushing her cheeks. "But we're going to be luckier than most people, Quenby, because we're both caretakers. We'll just take turns."

He didn't wait for a reply but shut the door softly behind him.

Quenby turned on her side so that she faced the window and could breathe in the lovely fragrances of the night.

Caretaker. What a lovely word, and how wonderful it would be to have someone who would cherish and care for you, not from duty but because it brought them joy.

She gazed into the darkness, not thinking, not

dreaming, somewhere between those two states until finally her lids grew heavy and then closed.

It was only while she was drifting down into the darkness of sleep that a troubled thought insinuated itself into the consciousness that was rapidly dancing away from her.

Gunner . . . when she had met him on the stairs he had been wearing a jacket.

Where had Gunner gone in the middle of the night?

Four

"I like to watch you sitting there playing the harp." Gunner leaned back on the cushioned love seat, stretching out his legs. "However, remind me to buy you something more appropriate to wear when you're entertaining me. The jeans and T-shirt tend to spoil the mood."

Quenby looked up and grinned, her fingers running over the strings. "A white robe and silver wings? You haven't listened to Vollenweider if you think the harp is confined to heavenly spheres."

"I have no desire for you to look angelic. I was thinking more along the lines of something medieval. You'd have been a lovely minstrel back in the olden days of romantic love when chivalry was in flower." His eyes narrowed on her face. "And rumors to the contrary, there was nothing angelic about the ladies of that period. I understand they were a lusty lot." He watched with enjoyment and mischief as her cheeks colored. "I'd much prefer you to follow in their footsteps, love."

She missed a chord and glanced at him in exasperation. It had been like this all day. Just when she was feeling comfortable and serene with the man, he said something that swiftly brought sexual awareness to the surface once more. He had been the perfect companion, teasing and joking one moment and then listening to her with a serious concentration that made her feel he was genuinely interested in every word she said. He possessed a sensitivity and understanding that made her feel as at ease with him as she would have in the presence of a good woman friend. She had never met a man who was both boldly aggressively and exquisitely sensitive.

But then, she had never met a man like Gunner Nilsen before, she thought. He was definitely in a class by himself.

Her hands fell away from the strings of the harp. "It's getting late. I think I'd better call Andrew in to take his bath and get ready for bed."

Gunner stood up. "I'll do it. Where is he?"

"On the bank of the stream with Steven. They're looking at the stars." She got to her feet. "And you will *not* do it. Every time I've started to do something today, you've jumped up and done it for me."

"I like to do things for you."

Quenby felt a melting deep inside her. *Caretaker.* "Well, if you don't let me do my job, I'm going to go crazy." She turned and walked briskly out of the parlor and down the hall toward the kitchen. "Andrew is so self-sufficient, there's little enough to do. Has he always been this independent?"

"Yep." Gunner had followed her and was now opening the screen door leading to the back porch. "Since the moment he was born he's never been anyone's person but his own. That's why our problem is complicated. Andrew is so damn strong."

"He's a little boy," Quenby said impatiently. "You're talking as if he were a grown man."

"Part of him is fully mature and that part has a responsibility—" He broke off as he caught sight of Steven and Andrew several yards distant. The small boy and the big man were sitting on the grassy bank, their faces lifted to the night sky. "But he *will* accept it."

"Responsibility?" Quenby asked as she followed him out on the porch and closed the screen door. "A five-year-old shouldn't have any responsibilities but behaving well and picking up his toys when he's finished with them."

Gunner's gaze was still on Andrew and Steven. "Andrew's responsibilities are a little more extensive than other children's. I told you he was extraordinary."

"Because he's gifted? I won't let you or anyone else pressure him," Quenby said fiercely. "He's a *child*, dammit."

"No one's pressuring him, or, if we are, it's for his own good." He dropped down on the white porch swing and stretched his legs out lazily. "Now, sit down and let me put my arm around you. I feel the need for some good old-fashioned spooning. This house has a very peculiar effect on me."

"But it's time for Andrew to go to bed."

"They look like they're enjoying themselves, and fifteen minutes more won't hurt anything. We'll just sit and swing and listen to the crickets. How long has it been since you sat on a porch swing and looked out at the night?"

"Years." Quenby slowly sat down beside him and his arm immediately went around her shoulders. There was nothing sexual in the embrace, it was only affectionate, comforting, caring. The night was warm and still, fireflies punctuating the darkness, stars blazing with a pure white fire in the deep midnight blue of the sky. Those stars seemed so close tonight, she thought dreamily. Not cold and distant as they were on some evenings. She leaned her head back on Gunner's arm and relaxed. "Too long."

"What a sensible lady. I should have known you'd realize that moments of beauty like this are more important than routine practicalities."

Quenby's gaze returned to Steven and Andrew. There was a beauty there too. A beauty as simple and uncomplicated as the night itself.

In the stillness, Steven's deep, eager voice drifted to them. "And that one up there is Centaurus. He's half man and half horse. Mr. Busby told me a witch made him that way when he tried to steal her cauldron away from her."

"I don't think that's right. The myth in the book I read—" Silence. "But books are wrong sometimes. What's that one there?"

"Leo, the lion. And there's the Big Dipper and the Little Dipper. Did you ever see anything so pretty, Andrew? Wouldn't you like to get on a spaceship and see them up close? I bet they'd be so bright and shiny they'd knock our eyes out."

"Up close they wouldn't sh—" Silence again. "Yes, I'd like to see them that way. But I like this too."

"So do I."

Fireflies flickered, disappeared in the darkness, and then flickered again. The only sounds to break the stillness were the creak of the porch swing and the soft splash of the wooden paddles as the wheel dipped into the waters of the stream.

"Andrew?"

"Hmmm?"

"Are you my friend?"

"Sure."

"Not for just now. Maybe for a long time?"

"Forever."

Another silence.

"I've never had a friend before. It's kinda . . . nice."

"I think so too."

"I don't know how long forever is."

"Long enough, Steven. Long enough."

Andrew's scream tore through the night.

Oh, dear, not again, Quenby thought frantically as she threw her covers back and jumped out of bed. The day had been so peaceful and happy and Andrew so contented she had felt sure the nightmares would not be repeated tonight. She grabbed her robe and ran for the door leading to the hall.

The door to Andrew's door was wide open and she saw that Gunner had already reached him. He was sitting on the side of Andrew's bed, wearing only a navy blue robe. His hands were grasping Andrew's shoulders and he was gazing intently into his eyes. "It's all right. There's nothing to fear, Andrew. Do you understand? I can help you."

Quenby knelt on the floor beside the bed. "Gunner's right. It was only a dream."

"No, it was real." Andrew's brown eyes were glittering with tears. "He was here."

"Shadows?" Gunner asked gently, one hand cupping Andrew's cheek. "I know all about the shadows. "I'll help you."

Andrew shook his head. "Not shadows. Not this time. A man . . ."

Quenby was conscious of an almost imperceptible stiffening of Gunner's body. "What man?"

"I don't know. I've never seen him before. His face was sort of twisted and he had funny jaws." He puffed out his cheeks. "Like a bulldog."

Gunner murmured something beneath his breath and then a more distinct, "Damn!"

"He's ugly, and he wants to hurt me." Andrew drew a quivering breath. "And he wants to hurt you, Gunner."

A faint smile curved Gunner's lips. "Then we'll just have to keep that from happening, won't we?" He suddenly stood up and lifted Andrew into his arms. "But now it's time for you to go back to sleep." He crossed to the rocking chair by the casement window and sat down with Andrew cradled in his arms. He began to rock back and forth. "I won't let anything hurt either of us."

"What about Quenby and Steven?"

"No one will be hurt." Gunner's long, graceful fingers stroked Andrew's temple. "Now, when I count to three, you're going to fall deeply asleep. You're not going to dream anymore tonight and you're going to wake up at eight o'clock in the morning rested and feeling well. Okay?"

"Okay."

"One."

Andrew cuddled contentedly closer.

"Two."

Gunner looked down at Andrew and a tender smile lit his face. "Three."

Andrew was asleep.

Quenby shook her head in amazement. "Will he truly not have any more nightmares tonight?"

Gunner nodded as he gave Andrew's slight body an affectionate hug. "Not tonight." He stood up and carried Andrew back to bed.

"Then why don't you tell him that every night?"

Gunner laid Andrew down and pulled the cover up to his chin. Andrew immediately turned over on his side and curled up.

"Because most of the time dreams are healthy."

"Even nightmares?"

"They offer a release we don't permit ourselves when we're awake. We all dream during the night, but we usually remember only the dream nearest wakening." His lips thinned. "Or the worst one."

"Well, Andrew has evidently been having quite a few 'worst' ones." Quenby got up from her kneeling position on the floor. "And I don't think it's one bit healthy." She whirled and strode toward the door. "And I don't believe you really do either or you wouldn't have told him he wasn't to dream anymore tonight."

"Tonight was different. I think he picked up something . . ." His expression was troubled. "I only hope he picked it up from me." He followed her, flicking off the overhead light and closing the door behind him. "It's entirely possible."

"I don't know what the devil you're talking about, but I'll be damned if I'll stand for this mysterious mumbo-jumbo any longer. Tomorrow I'm going to call Andrew's mother and have a long talk with her. If she and Andrew are as close as you claim, then she'll tell me what I need to know to help him."

"You can't do that."

"The hell I can't. Try and stop me." Quenby turned on her heel and strode the short distance down the hall to her own room. "I won't stand by while Andrew is tortured like this every night."

Gunner followed her. "You'd only worry her. All of this is hard enough for Elizabeth without your making matters more difficult."

"I'm not making matters more difficult." Quenby threw open the door and turned to face him. "I'm going to simplify things."

"We're so close— Dammit, Quenby, trust me just a little longer."

"No," she said succinctly. "Good night, Gunner."

Gunner was silent for a long moment. "Okay." He took a step closer. "You want it, you'll get it.

No more secrets." He reached out for the switch on the wall beside the door and turned on the overhead light. In the sudden illumination she saw an expression of coldness mingled with stormy anger she had never before seen on Gunner's face. "Go sit down," he ordered her.

Quenby found to her surprise that she was meekly obeying him. She sat down in the pale blue wing chair beside the bed, her back straight, her bare feet close together on the carpet. "I don't see why you're so angry. I'm the one who's been kept in the dark and treated like a half-wit."

"I'm angry because I'm hurt, dammit. I wanted you to trust me." His sapphire-blue eyes were blazing at her as he slammed the door before crossing the room and sitting down on the bed. "And because it's too soon for you to believe me and you'll probably think I'm bonkers."

"I've suspected you were around the bend since I first saw you dashing across those runways dodging machine-gun bullets."

"That was necessary."

"That was madness." Quenby glared at him, remembering that episode with fresh poignancy. If one of those bullets had hit him, she would never have known him. He would just have been a beautiful stranger cut down tragically in his youth. But now she *did* know him, blast it, and reliving that moment scared her to death. "You had no right to take chances like that."

"It's my choice."

"Is it? Not when—" Quenby drew a deep breath. "Andrew. Tell me about Andrew."

He gazed at her moodily. "You're not going to believe me."

"Tell me."

"Andrew is Elizabeth's son, but Jon is actually Andrew's stepfather. Elizabeth doesn't belong to the Clanad but was formerly married to another member of the Clanad, Mark Ramsey. Andrew's the only child born of such a union so far." His lips twisted. "I told you we Garvanians have a passion for reason. Most of us try to avoid the problems a union like Elizabeth and Mark's poses."

"I want to know about Andrew, not about the members of your corporation."

"The Clanad isn't a corporation. It's a group of fifty-three individuals who underwent a scientific experiment a number of years ago in Garvania. We were given a rare chemical from a plant that's now extinct." He drew a deep breath. "It . . . changed us. You've probably heard that a human being uses only about ten percent of the capacity of his brain. Well, mirandite gave us the ability to tap an additional thirty to fifty percent. That doesn't mean we're particularly cerebral, it just means we can learn practically anything and our problem-solving abilities are correspondingly magnified."

Quenby sat frozen. She wanted to laugh but she was too surprised. This was nonsense, something from a science fiction movie.

"There's something else." He paused. "With mind expansion came certain talents and skills. We're telepaths, Quenby."

She did laugh then. A very uncertain laugh. "This is crazy."

"I knew you'd say that, dammit."

"What do you expect me to say? I've never heard such an outlandish story in my life."

"Well, you're going to hear the rest of it." Gunner's expression was grim. "It all came in one package: Telepathy, mind control, some of us are even psychokinetic. That's the reason we formed into a group under the protection of the Sheikh Ben Raschid. We had to develop firm control procedures to make sure we wouldn't hurt society. We developed those psychological controls, Quenby. There's absolutely no question we would hurt anyone by intruding upon their privacy. To do that would hurt us far more than it would them."

"And Andrew is telepathic too?" Quenby's voice was disbelieving.

"Yes, it was inherited from his father, but he has an increased sensitivity because of Elizabeth and—"

"I can't listen to any more of this." She jumped to her feet. "I've never heard such a complete cock and bull story in my life. Why did you think I'd swallow such a wild tale?"

"I didn't believe it." He rose to his feet. "I told you it was too soon. You still intend to call Elizabeth?"

"Of course. Maybe she'll be truthful with me. I'm sure she'll at least not insult my intelligence with a fabrication like this."

A flicker of anger flared in his eyes. "I can't let you worry Elizabeth, Quenby."

"Are you going to disconnect the phone?"

"No." He stood looking at her. "I guess I'll just have to convince you that what I've told you is true."

She gazed at him incredulously. "Good luck!"

"Oh, I won't need luck." His smile was bittersweet. "I could have used a little trust, but I've learned to do without luck." He turned toward the door. "Have a good night, Quenby."

A moment later the door closed behind him.

Quenby gazed at the panels of the door, hurt, bewilderment and anger surging through her in a wildly jumbled flow. Trust? Why hadn't he trusted her? Why had he tried to mock her with this wild explanation? His former refusal to confide in her was kinder than this.

She strode across the room and turned out the light. A moment later she was in bed, pulling the covers over her. She firmly blinked back tears, swallowing to ease the tightness in her throat. She willed herself to go to sleep. She would not lie here thinking about Gunner and his foolish story. It was fortunate she had learned how little respect he had for her intelligence so early in their relationship.

And he had actually had the colossal nerve to be angry when she hadn't believed the story he had fabricated.

Oh, damn, why couldn't he have been honest with her?

It had to be a dream.

Quenby stirred restlessly, settling herself beneath the covers. There was no question that the secret, delicious sensations she was experiencing were rooted in her hallucination. Strange. She had never been prone to erotic dreams before. . . .

She shivered with intense pleasure as the large gentle hands stroking her breasts suddenly cupped and then began squeezing gently, rhythmically. Her spine arched mindlessly upward and she was aware that her breath was coming in little gasps. Heat seared through her as she felt Gunner's tongue on her nipples.

Gunner? How had Gunner intruded into her dream? She had been conscious only of touch and masculinity, but now she realized with utter certainty that this touch was Gunner's and the masculinity was both bold and aroused. His teeth were closing on one taut nipple, biting gently. A flash of hot electricity enveloped her, ending in a throbbing yearning between her thighs.

"Roll over, love." Gunner's voice.

No, not really a voice, she thought dreamily. There was no sound. . . .

"That's right. You're so sweet like this. Now open your thighs and let me come in."

Why not? It was only a dream and she was aching. Empty.

"You want it, love? Ah, I see you do. Do you realize how wonderful it makes me feel to know I can give you pleasure?" Fingers. Long, masculine fingers, teasing, searching.

Quenby's nails dug into the mattress. This was so *real*. Her head thrashed back and forth on the pillow. Too real. Entering ... in ... out ... around. She bit her lower lip to keep a scream from tumbling out. She mustn't wake now. She was so close. . . . The fingers quickened. There was suddenly a mouth on her breast, suckling strongly.

"Let it happen, love." Gunner's soundless voice, soft, loving. "I want to pleasure you. Relax and let me give you what you need."

Fever. Emptiness. Gunner.

Her heart was racing so fast, she thought she would faint. Her tongue moistened her lips. "Gunner," she whispered. "It's hurting." It was true, the desire and hunger were painful in their intensity. "I can't—"

What was she doing?

The sound of her own voice had jarred her from sleep. The suckling at her breast continued, and so did Gunner's rhythmic fingers. This was insane. What was happening to her?

A hesitance. Then Gunner's soundless voice. "Rats."

An instant later Gunner was gone. Or rather, the sensations he was causing were gone. She was empty, throbbing, incomplete. Only a dream. An insane, wildly erotic dream. Her heart was still throbbing crazily, and she was hot and trembling. It had seemed so real.

She turned over on her side. Why would she have an erotic dream about Gunner when she had been so angry with him? That was even more bewildering than the dream itself. It was completely unlike her and totally without precedent.

Unless Gunner had hypnotized her.

Her eyes flicked open in the darkness.

She lay there, stunned by the possibility that had occurred to her. Yet it could be true. Gunner was an accomplished hypnotist; she had seen that herself. What if he had managed to plant a hypnotic suggestion in some way? No, she had to be wrong. She hadn't permitted him to hypnotize her. Could someone be hypnotized without their knowing it? She had seen a horror movie once on the late, late show . . .

Oh, how did she know? She knew very little about hypnosis, but she was beginning to believe she *had* been an unwilling subject.

A flash of anger burned through her. How had he dared to do that to her? It must have seemed very funny to him. A big joke played on a gullible woman who had been terribly close to falling in love.

She sat up in bed and tossed the covers aside, swinging her feet to the floor. She didn't take the time to switch on the lamp as she stood up, nor did she bother to slip on a robe to cover the silky golden tap pants and matching camisole she was wearing. She merely grabbed the thermos carafe of ice water on the bedside table, and stalked across the room toward the door.

Five

A few seconds later she was throwing open the door to Gunner's room. It was dark in the room, but she could barely discern the outline of the double bed against the far wall.

"Quenby?" It was Gunner's voice. The same voice that had invaded her dream, but now the tone held not seduction but wariness.

He had better be wary, she thought as she strode toward the bed. She was angry enough to draw and quarter him. "Of course it's me. Didn't you expect me to pay you a visit?"

"Yes, I did but—"

"Perhaps you thought I'd come running to jump into bed with you." She was beside the bed and saw that Gunner was sitting up, naked to the waist, the sheet draped across his hips. "Well, I came running all right. I don't like being hypnotized against my will. I don't know how you did it, but I'm sure you managed it somehow. *Damn you, Gunner Nilsen!*"

She held out the carafe and poured a stream of ice water over Gunner's naked chest and shoulders.

Gunner yelped with shock as the ice water ran down his chest and soaked the sheets. "Hell, Quenby, it was meant for the best. Lord, that's *cold*." As he jumped out of bed and flicked on the lamp Quenby caught a disturbing glimpse of tight lean buttocks before he disappeared into the adjoining bathroom. He left the bathroom door open and she could hear him growling half beneath his breath. "You Swedes may be accustomed to ice baths, but Garvania is a desert country." He turned on the bathroom light and ran a large white bath towel over his chest and long powerful legs. "That was damn unpleasant."

The sudden tingling she was feeling was only a remnant left over from that erotic dream, she assured herself quickly. "No more unpleasant than what you did to me."

He tossed the towel aside and reached for another to tie around his hips. "You thought what I did to you was very pleasant at the time." He scowled. "I couldn't help it if you woke up before I finished. I know it must have been very frustrating, but that wasn't my fault."

Her eyes widened. "How did you know I woke up before . . ." She moistened her lips nervously. "A guess. You must be very good at this hypnosis business."

"I am good." He walked toward her. "But it

wasn't hypnosis this time. It was telepathy. I waited until you were asleep and projected images and sensations into your subconscious."

She laughed uncertainly. "Are you on that track again? I told you I didn't believe—"

She gasped. The gentle, sensual probing between her thighs was unmistakable, but Gunner was standing four feet away! "I'm going crazy."

Gunner shook his head. The sensual probing faded away and she received the impression of Gunner's poignant reluctance to leave her. "Sorry about that. But I had to show you I could do it while you were fully awake. The only reason I came in the back door of sleep was that I knew it was going to come as a shock and I wanted to ease you into it."

"Ease me into it!" Her cheeks glowed with color. "You call mentally raping me easing—"

"I didn't rape you. I seduced you," he said quickly. "I made sure you knew who I was, and if your subconscious had had any objections, it would have closed me out. Your subconscious knows you're mine even if your conscious mind is still confused about it. And I only played around a little and tried to give you pleasure. I didn't actually . . ." He paused and made a face. "Though I can't say I was being noble. I was saving the real thing for a time when I could enjoy it too." His voice became low. "I had to convince you, Quenby. I just did it in a way that would give you the most pleasure."

She shook her head. He was telling her the truth. There was no doubt in her mind that he was absolutely sincere, and if what he was saying was true . . . "You're asking me to believe all that nonsense you told me is the truth?"

"I asked you to believe me before, and you didn't do it." His lips curved in a bittersweet smile. "I guess I was hurt enough to want to prove myself, so I provided a demonstration. I think it worked. You do believe me now, don't you, Quenby?"

Incredibly, she was beginning to believe every word he had said. Her knees suddenly felt weak, and she sank into the chair beside the bed. "I think perhaps I am. I must be going bananas."

"Good." He breathed a sigh of relief. "I'm glad that's over. I was cursing that stubbornness of yours, but maybe it was all for the best. Now that we've reached an understanding, we can move on to the business of getting to know each other."

She looked at him warily. "If you call what you did to me reaching an understanding, I'd like to know what you call intimacy."

"Oh, that's minor," Gunner said breezily. "And don't worry, it was just a demonstration. I won't intrude again without your permission."

"How could you do it this time? I thought you said your people had rules about things like that."

"We do, but there are exceptions. We have permission to use our skills in case of life endangerment or to help someone in desperate need—"

"I don't fall into either of those categories."

"But there's another exception that you do fall under." Gunner's voice was soft. "We can enter the mind of our *valon*."

"*Valon?*"

"It's a Garvanian word. It means the"—he paused, searching for an exact explanation—"it's difficult to translate. 'Souls entwined' comes closest. The one who shares your soul. You're my *valon*, Quenby. I knew it the moment I saw you."

She gazed at him, her mind whirling. She tried to laugh. "How many times a year do you run across a *valon?*"

A shadow of pain flitted across his face. "Don't laugh. This happens once in a lifetime, Quenby."

"How can I believe that? How can I believe anything you say? You march into my life and turn me inside out. You play games with my mind and claim you have a perfect right to do it because we're some kind of soulmates." She ran her fingers through her hair. "I don't like any of this one bit. I like everything clear and open and down-to-earth." She glared at him. "And I'm not at all sure my subconscious gave you permission to do anything. How do I know you're telling me the truth? You evidently can twist my thinking any way you please."

"Will it help if I promise you that I won't come into your mind unless I'm invited?"

"Will you do that?"

He nodded. "I won't promise to keep out indefinitely, but I'll let you get accustomed to the idea first. I think that's fair." He smiled wistfully. "I like being inside your mind, Quenby. It's clean and beautiful and more comfortable than anyone else's I've ever entered. I wanted to curl up and stay awhile."

Her laugh held a hint of desperation. "I'm a soft, cushy pillow and my mind's 'comfortable.' If all this weren't so bizarre, I'd be insulted."

He frowned. "Why? It's wonderful to be able to bring peace and tranquility to those around you."

"Because I . . ." She trailed off in frustration. She didn't want him to think of her as "comfortable." She was quite sure he hadn't looked for such a trait in that what's-her-name who had been his last mistress. She would bet the lady had leaned more toward *exciting* rather than comfortable.

"Her name was Mary Ann," Gunner said absently. "And you're ten times more exciting than she ever was."

A ripple of shock went through her. "You . . . you peeked!"

"Just one last time," he admitted sheepishly. "I couldn't resist. I had to make sure you still wanted me. This situation is a big shock to you, and some women might find it revolting." A cloud darkened his expression. "Might find *me* revolting. I know I'm something of a freak."

"I don't find you revolting." Her eyes were blazing. "But I do find you completely unprincipled. You promised me you'd stay out of my mind, blast you." She turned on her heel and strode toward the door.

"Where are you going?"

"I'm going to pack my suitcases. I won't stay here and be subjected to a peeping Tom who has no conscience at all."

He reached the door before she did and stood in front of it. "I slipped. It won't happen again. It was just so damn important for me to know you're not disgusted with me." He frowned like a sulky little boy. "So I'm not perfect. You can still trust me."

"Let me pass."

"Look, do you want to come in and take a peek at my mind? I can let you do it. Then you'll see I can be trusted."

Would he really permit her to violate his privacy in this most personal of trespasses? His gaze was perfectly guileless, he meant every word he had said. She glanced away. "No, thank you. I don't think I'm prepared to go mind-dipping."

"Then trust me. It won't happen again." Gunner's voice was convincing. "It was an impulse. I acted without thinking."

"You seem to do that quite frequently," she said dryly. "What assurance do I have that it won't happen again?"

"None," he said frankly. "But I'm not as devoid of conscience as you may believe. I keep my word."

"When you think about it."

He grimaced. "I stand corrected. I told you I wasn't perfect."

She lifted her gaze to his face. No, he wasn't perfect and he would make mistakes. She suddenly felt a great surge of relief pour through her. Gunner might possess a superintelligence, but he was vulnerable and insecure enough to worry about how he appeared in her eyes.

Why, she had actually been afraid of him, she realized. She hadn't been conscious of the fear, but it had been present from the moment she had accepted his words as truth. Great power resided in the concept he had introduced to her, and power inevitably bred fear. But her instinct told her there was nothing to fear in Gunner.

He was looking intently at her. "You'll stay?"

"You're not reading my mind again?" She gazed at him suspiciously.

His face lit with joyous relief. "No, I promise." He took a step closer. "You're going to stay!" He picked her up and whirled her around in a circle. "Damn, you had me scared."

"Gunner, put me down." Her hands clutched wildly at his bare shoulders. A deep vibration seemed to pierce her palms and spread up to her wrists. He was smooth and warm and golden, pulsing with vitality and virility beneath her hands.

"Anything you say." His dark-blue eyes were alive with mischief as he slowly slid her down his body, letting her feel every muscle. He was aroused. "Sure you don't want to come in and find out what I'm thinking?" he whispered. "You'd like it. I'll tell you anyway. I'm thinking how nice it would be to get rid of that silky bit of nothing you're almost wearing. Then I could rub against you and feel how soft and hot you are. Then I'd put my hand—"

"Hush!" She swallowed, her cheeks scarlet. "I don't want to go into your mind and I don't want you to tell me. Let me go."

He didn't obey immediately, his narrowed gaze

on her face. "Oh, all right." He reluctantly released her and stepped back. "If you insist."

"I insist." She tried to steady her voice. "Just because I've agreed to stay is no reason to assume I'm going to rush into a relationship with you."

"There's no rush about it. I keep telling you, we've been heading toward each other ever since the moment we were born." He smiled gently. "But I can see that you need time to pull all the loose ends together in your head. I'll give you a day or so to get used to the idea."

"How generous of you."

"Did that sound arrogant? I didn't mean it to be. I meant only that you're bright and clear-thinking and it won't take you long to assimilate everything I've told you and come to the same conclusion I did."

"And what is that?"

"That I'm your *valon*," he said simply. "Forever."

Tears misted her eyes and she felt something give, then crumble and dissolve as she looked at him. She was very much afraid she was coming to that conclusion right now. It was impossible. How could she have come to this point of no return with a man who would bring her nothing but a myriad of problems she could only dimly envision? But she hadn't passed that point yet. Not yet.

She drew a deep, quivering breath. She couldn't cope with this now. She was too bewildered and raw from this night's bombardment of emotions. "I want to go to bed now and I have no desire to discuss this again until I've had time to think it over."

He nodded slowly. "That's reasonable. Not much fun but definitely reasonable."

"And there's something else I do want to discuss. Andrew's problem."

The amusement vanished from Gunner's expression. "I was going to tell you about that but you wouldn't listen."

"I'm listening now." She turned and moved quickly across the room to where Gunner's blue terrycloth robe was lying over the back of the chair. She definitely needed to put something between them even if it was only a layer of material. "You said Andrew is a telepath too?"

He nodded. "A very strong telepath. It appears the joining with a nonclanad mind served to intensify the potential." He paused. "But unfortunately it also increased his sensitivity. The members of the Clanad found it relatively easy to learn to erect barriers to keep out unwelcome static but—"

"Static?"

"Fragments of thoughts of those around us," Gunner clarified. "Usually there's no problem, but a sudden flare-up of emotion or violence in anyone in the immediate area sometimes filters through the barrier."

"And Andrew couldn't acquire this barrier?"

"He was learning. I was chosen to teach him and he *was* learning. We were careful to keep him away from anyone but the Clanad so that he wasn't exposed to anything that might hurt him." He paused. "But about a year ago something happened that we didn't expect. One of the members of the Clanad had an automobile accident. He crashed into an embankment on the grounds of the compound and his car broke into flames. He died fifteen minutes later in great pain."

"And Andrew . . ." Quenby couldn't force the rest of the words from her lips. "My God, the poor baby."

Gunner nodded grimly. "He couldn't close it out. He felt both the man's agony and his death. He was hysterical for almost two days and we couldn't do anything to help him. Jon and Elizabeth went through hell. They thought he might go insane." His eyes were haunted. "And I blamed myself. I was taking my time teaching him. I thought it would be better to go slow than initiate a crash course that might possibly be a shock to his psyche."

"It was reasonable to think that," Quenby said gently. "No one could know the accident would happen."

"I should have known." His voice held a note of savagery as well as pain. "I know how much violence there is in the world. I shouldn't have left him vulnerable."

"But he got better," she said soothingly. "He appears almost entirely normal except for those nightmares. Is it the accident he dreams about?"

Gunner shook his head. "No."

"Then what?"

"After the hysterics Andrew went into an almost catatonic withdrawal for over a week. Then one day he opened his eyes and seemed completely normal. He appeared to have forgotten everything that had happened. Lord, we were all so damn happy that we were over the moon. We thought he had somehow managed to heal himself and everything was going to be all right."

"But it wasn't?"

"No, he had healed himself, but he had also done something else. He had erected his own barrier against the pain and, because Andrew is strong, his defensive action was correspondingly strong. He not only shut out the static but everything else too. He's hiding behind that barrier and rejecting the fact that he's a telepath."

"Maybe that's healthy," Quenby suggested. "After what he's suffered, I don't think I'd want him to regain a talent with that potential for danger."

"That's the way Elizabeth felt. She didn't give a damn if he ever became anything more than what he was." He paused. "Until the nightmares started. At first he was having them just once every so often, then more frequently, and finally every night. He became afraid to close his eyes."

"Did you take him to a psychiatrist?"

"He was under the Clanad's best medical care from the night of the accident. They didn't know what the hell to do either." He smiled crookedly. "There aren't many precedents for most of the problems facing us. It's hit or miss and then pray. However, they finally came up with a diagnosis and a possible solution. Andrew is a *natural* telepath, and this suppression is completely unnatural for him. His mind is a battleground, and the only time he lets himself be conscious of that battle is when he goes to sleep."

"And the shadows?"

"The shadows are thoughts trying to get past the barrier. Thoughts he's afraid of accepting because they may contain the same shock and pain that nearly drove him insane."

It made sense, and Quenby felt again that deep pang of aching sympathy for Andrew. "Did you try hypnosis?"

"He'll let me go so far and no further."

"Then what can you do?"

"Find a way to tear down the barrier."

"No!" Her rejection came instantly. "You can't want him to go through that pain again."

"Of course I don't. I'd rather he stayed as he is right now than go through that trauma again. Do you think I'm a monster?"

"I didn't mean—"

"He's getting worse," Gunner said curtly. "The mind has a very fragile balance, and we don't dare leave the barrier as it is. Once it tumbles, I can help Andrew face what happened and build another barrier that he can control."

"And how are you going to get through?"

"I'm hoping he'll do it himself," Gunner said. "Andrew has always been a very loving child with the instincts of a healer. It's one of his most prominent characteristics."

It suddenly occurred to Quenby where he was leading. "Steven is the catalyst you were speaking about. You threw the two of them together so that Andrew would try to help Steven."

"Not try," Gunner said quietly. "Andrew can

heal Steven. We've been studying the varying degrees of intelligence for the last five years and there are things we can do, ways we can help open up new paths to people like Steven. We can teach them by actually *showing* them concepts. We're not sure how far we can go yet, but we know we can help. It takes time and effort and is a great strain on the telepath, but we can go in and make great inroads."

"How wonderful," Quenby said. "It's a miracle."

"No, just a new science. Unfortunately we're still learning the dos and don'ts of the procedure."

"What if Andrew can't force himself to help Steven?"

Gunner's lips tightened. "Then I'll take Andrew and Steven back to Sedikhan. I'll turn Steven over to the Clanad to help with his problems and try to think of something else that will help Andrew."

"But you don't have much hope of finding an alternative."

"I always have hope. I just don't know . . ." He shrugged. "But maybe that won't be necessary. Lord, I hope not. Andrew and Steven are definitely forming an attachment to each other. You could see that tonight."

Her throat tightened as she remembered the man and the boy on the banks of the stream, their gazes lifted to the stars. "Yes, they're growing very close."

"Help me, Quenby?" Gunner was pleading. "Help Andrew to get well. I'm going to need you. I don't know what to expect when he comes to the point of no return."

Strange that Gunner should choose the same phrase she had mentally used earlier. Both Andrew and she were sailing into very hazardous waters, and there was no question that she'd be there to help him even though she could not seem to help herself. "I intend to help Andrew. That's why I'm here. Is there anything else I should know?"

He hesitated and seemed about to speak. Then he shook his head slowly. "Not now. I've given you enough to think about tonight. I'll let you sleep on this and then go into the rest of the situation tomorrow."

She didn't argue with him. She was abruptly experiencing a numbing exhaustion. "Tomorrow." She crossed the room and opened the door. "Good night, Gunner."

"Quenby."

She glanced inquiringly over her shoulder.

"It's not just Andrew, is it? I know you want to help the boy, but it's not only that." His words were raw, awkward. "I mean, it's me, too, isn't it? You want to stay and get to know me."

She hesitated. He was asking too much of her right now. She should give him a sharp setdown. She opened her mouth to do just that but made the mistake of meeting his pleading, vulnerable . . . loving gaze. How could you administer a kick to a man who looked at you like that?

She sighed. "Yes, Gunner, I want to get to know you too." She turned away as she saw the sunlight break over his troubled face. "But not quite as quickly or intimately as you obviously have in mind. Stay out of my dreams, dammit!"

The door clicked shut firmly behind her.

It was twenty minutes later, as Quenby was drifting off to sleep, that she heard Gunner's footsteps pass her door and then continue down the stairs.

Another mystery Gunner had not seen fit to confide in her, she thought drowsily. She must remember to ask him about these nocturnal wanderings. . . .

Six

"I want to buy Steven a present." Andrew finished off the last bite of his pancakes and pushed away his plate. "A birthday present."

Gunner set the carafe of coffee back on the warmer and leaned back in his chair. "Have the two of you decided on which day you want to celebrate his birthday?"

Andrew nodded. "May twenty-second. That's four days from now. Is that okay?"

"It sounds like a fine day for a birthday," Quenby said. "What kind of present were you thinking of buying for Steven?"

Andrew frowned. "I don't know, something to do with stars. Maybe a big book with lots of pictures. I don't think Steven knows how to read very well."

"Something to do with stars . . ." Quenby's brow knitted in thought. "I think I may have an idea."

"What is it?" Andrew's face lit with eagerness. "Will he like it?"

"Oh, yes, I'm sure he'll like it." Quenby leaned forward and brushed the top of his golden head with her lips. He was as bright and shining this morning as if the near hysteria of last night had never taken place. Thank heaven for the resilience of the very young. "But I'm not sure it can be arranged by Steven's birthday. Let me make a phone call and get back to you later today."

"Is it better than a book?"

"Much better than a book," Quenby assured him as she stood up. "But if we're going to have a birthday party, you're going to have to ask Steven what kind of cake and ice cream he likes. Then we'll have to go into town and get balloons and party favors and—"

"I'll find out." Andrew jumped to his feet, his brown eyes shining with excitement. "It's going to be a terrific party, isn't it, Quenby? May I go tell Steven right now?"

"I don't see why not. Where is he? Didn't you tell him we wanted him to have his meals with us?"

"I told him." Andrew was already at the screen door. "But he wanted to start work on the treehouse as soon as it got light this morning."

"He still has to eat. Bring him back—" Quenby stopped and sighed in resignation. She was talking to the air; Andrew was gone.

Gunner laughed. "Don't worry, I'll take a picnic

lunch out to them in the woods." He got to his feet with seeming casualness and strolled to the screen door, watching Andrew as he hurried across the meadow toward the woods. "By the way, Jon thought we might need a little help with Andrew, so he sent Judd Walker to keep an eye on him while he's in the woods with Steven. I picked Judd up last night at the airport and dropped him off at a motel in town, but he'll be drifting around the premises every day from now on. Judd's black, about thirty-five, tall and slim. He'll try to be as unobtrusive as possible, but you might catch a glimpse of him now and then and I didn't want you to imagine he was any threat to Andrew."

Quenby looked up from stacking dishes. "Why on earth should I need any help? I don't have enough to do as it is. How many nannies does Andrew need?"

"Judd isn't exactly that kind of help."

"Just what kind of help is he?"

"Jon is a very rich and powerful man. Naturally he wants to make sure Andrew is safe."

Quenby stopped stacking the dishes and very deliberately sat back down in her chair. "Safe? You're talking about bodyguards."

"I didn't say—"

"I'm not dense," Quenby said crisply. "And I'm quite accustomed to the necessity for hiring bodyguards to protect the children of the rich and the famous. Unfortunately there are some sickos out there who wouldn't hesitate to hurt a child to gain money or revenge. Now, stop trying to protect me from the hideous shock of realizing Andrew is one of those children and tell me why this Judd Walker has been called in to help you. You're quite competent to handle most ordinary problems, so it follows that there must be an extraordinary one on the horizon. Is that correct?"

"I didn't think you were dense, quite the contrary. I just didn't want you to worry for no reason. Andrew may be perfectly safe."

"Then where do you go in the middle of the night?" Quenby met his gaze. "Steven and Andrew may be into stargazing, but I doubt anything so innocent is what's keeping you on the prowl."

"No, it's not. You're going to pin me to the wall on this, aren't you?"

"You're darn right. Has Andrew safely reached the woods? I assume that's why you're standing there watching him."

Gunner nodded. "Steven saw him and came to meet him."

"And this Judd person is presumably watching both of them." Quenby poured herself another cup of coffee. "Come and sit down. You have some explaining to do."

"Why do I feel I'm about to be spanked?" Gunner's eyes were twinkling as he meekly obeyed her. "I fully intended to tell you about this."

"Eventually." Quenby's tone was dry. "I don't like to be kept in the dark, and I'm fully capable of making my own judgments about what's good for me. Is someone trying to kidnap Andrew?"

"No." Gunner reached for the glass coffeepot

and poured more coffee into his cup. "At least I don't think so."

"Then why are you worried?"

"I'm not exactly worried. I'm just being cautious. Andrew is in my keeping, and I don't want anything to happen to him."

"Gunner, if you don't stop these evasions . . ."

Gunner looked down into the depths of his coffee cup. "The first day we came here I sensed something. It was only for a split-second and I could have been wrong. I thought someone was watching us from the woods on the other side of the road."

A chill ran down Quenby's spine. "Even if you were right, it could have been someone perfectly innocent."

"No, it was more—" He lifted his gaze. "I thought it was Karl Bardot."

"Who's Karl Bardot?"

"He was the head of a secret government agency a number of years ago. The National Intelligence Bureau was staffed by people whose tactics were both arbitrary and unprincipaled and made CIA agents seem like pussycats by comparison. The agency was evaluated and disbanded about four years ago, and Karl Bardot dropped from sight."

"Why should he be interested in Andrew?"

"Five years ago Bardot was investigating the Clanad. We were based here in the States at the time." Gunner's expression was grim. "Bardot claimed we were all freaks and a danger to the government. He became fanatical on the subject and after Andrew was born—" He paused. "He claimed he only wanted to study Andrew, but at one point he threatened to shoot him."

"Kill a helpless baby?" Quenby felt sickened.

"He wasn't rational. I think he would have murdered us all if he'd gotten the chance."

"But you managed to defeat him?"

"Jon found a way to discredit Bardot, who was dismissed from the NIB. We kept an eye on him, but after the entire Clanad moved to Sedikhan, we somehow lost track of him."

"And you think this Bardot might be watching the house?" The very idea terrified her. "After all this time?"

"I don't *know*, dammit. I could be wrong. I told you I'm not perfect." Gunner seemed to Quenby to be under great strain. "But, if I am right, it isn't kidnapping we have to worry about."

"Murder?" Quenby's voice was only a wisp of a sound.

Gunner nodded slowly. "Bardot has an ugliness inside him. We have to make sure he never gets his hands on Andrew. That's why Jon sent Judd to help watch over him. Judd's a member of the Clanad and he would be able to sense Bardot's presence even if he weren't in sight."

"But you said you could be wrong. Have you been conscious of his presence since that first day?"

"No, for the past two nights I've gone into the woods and searched. There's been no trace of him. Perhaps he's gone away." He shrugged wearily. "Or perhaps he was never there."

Quenby drew a deep breath. "Is there anything else I should know?"

"Only Bardot's description. You should be able to recognize him if you see him. He's in his forties with thinning gray hair and heavy bulldog jowls."

"Heavy jowls." Her eyes widened. "The man Andrew dreamed about."

"Probably. But he may have picked it up from me as static. It's possible."

"Or he may have picked it up from Karl Bardot." Quenby swallowed to ease the tightness of her throat. "But the emotional thrust, the hatred, would have to be terribly strong to pierce through that barrier Andrew's erected, wouldn't it?"

"Yes." Gunner's voice was very soft. "It would have to be exceptionally strong, Quenby."

She shivered. She didn't want to think of Bardot and his poisonous hatred leveled at a helpless little boy.

Gunner reached out and gently touched her cheek with his finger. "It will be all right. Together we'll protect him. If there's even a hint that Bardot's around, I'll send you all to Sedikhan, where you'll be safe."

"And what will you do?"

Something reckless and wild flickered in the blue eyes gazing into her own. "If it's Bardot, it would be irresponsible of me to let him walk around, a danger to all of us. I think I'd go hunting."

She gazed at him in horror. He meant it. He'd just told her that Bardot had wanted to murder not only Andrew but the entire Clanad, and yet he'd blithely go after him, risking his life without a thought. "Irresponsible? When have you ever been anything else? You *want* to go after him." Her eyes blazed up at him. "You'd enjoy it. It would be some kind of kick for you." She pushed her chair back with such violence it made a scraping noise on the parquet floor. "Go away. I don't want to see you for a while." She stood up and resumed stacking the dishes. "I may not want to see you ever again. Lord, you're an idiot."

"Quenby—"

"Did you hear me? Go away!" Her voice was trembling but she refused to look at him. "Go play with the other children." She began to load the dishwasher. "Maybe they'll understand that kind of reasoning, but I don't."

"You're afraid for me." Gunner's voice was filled with delight. "You're actually worried about me."

"Why should I be—" She stopped and closed her eyes. Damn, she wanted to murder him herself. "I'm sure it's a temporary aberration that I'll do everything in my power to correct."

"Quenby, open your eyes." He was beside her. "You won't let me peek inside, and I want to see what you're feeling."

"Go to hell." Her voice broke on the last word. Her eyes remained tightly shut. "Go anywhere. Just get away from me."

Gunner was silent, hesitating, then she heard him move away from her. "I'm going, but I have an idea this is a mistake. My instincts tell me to rush in and consolidate my gains."

"You haven't gained anything."

"The hell I haven't." Gunner was jubilant. "You must feel something for me or you wouldn't be so furious with me." The screen door opened. "Whoopee!"

The screen door slammed shut behind him and she heard him laughing as he ran down the back porch steps.

Quenby's lids flicked open to reveal eyes swimming with tears she'd refused to shed. Damn him, she thought desperately, she didn't want him to be right. She had no desire to let anyone have the power to frighten her like this. Particularly a man who regarded danger as a pleasant pastime and didn't have the sense to be frightened by machine-gun bullets or crazy men.

The tears were running down her cheeks now, and she reached out and pulled a paper towel from the rack under the cabinet. And to cap it off, the man was a bloody telepath too. Who knew what he would spring on her next? She didn't *want* to love Gunner Nilsen.

Love. The word filled her with panic. She had so carefully kept the concept submerged that it had taken the thought of Gunner in danger to bring it springing to the forefront. She couldn't love him. They had met such a short time ago, and there were so many obstacles in their path.

But dear Lord, she *did* love him!

She walked slowly over to the back door and gazed out through the screen. Gunner was crossing the meadow, the sunlight forming a nimbus around his golden head, his step springy, his lithe, strong body brimming with vitality. He shouted something laughingly to someone out of her line of vision in the woods and waved with an exuberance that filled Quenby with tenderness. He was so alive, so open and outgoing, so damn loving and lovable. How could a woman be expected to resist him?

Well, she had certainly fallen with a resounding thud, she thought gloomily. After her disastrous relationship with Raoul, she had sworn she would be involved only with men who were both rock-solid and sensible. No one who had an ounce of judgment would say Gunner was either.

No, she was far from pleased about her foolishness in falling in love with Gunner Nilsen.

He was walking a tightrope.

Quenby stopped short, her eyes on Gunner's figure balanced on the rope strung between the branches of two giant maple trees. The picnic basket she was carrying fell to the ground from her nerveless hand. The rope tied to the limbs was at least forty feet from the ground. One misstep could bring almost certain injury or death. She was afraid to speak, afraid to breathe.

Gunner was nearly halfway to the other tree, his stocking feet moving with careful surety over the taut slenderness of the rope. He was laughing, his face alight with the same recklessness she had seen only a few hours ago.

"Quenby!" Andrew's whisper came form the lowest limb of the tree a few feet from where she was standing. "Isn't it neat? Just like a real circus.

Steven said he'd never been to a circus, so Gunner told him—"

"Shh." She was desperately afraid Gunner's attention would be distracted and he would come crashing to the ground. "Later, Andrew."

Gunner was almost to the tree that was his objective, and she found herself praying beneath her breath. Don't let him fall. Oh, God, don't let him be hurt.

Then he reached the safety of the other tree and hopped from the rope to the dubious security of a thick, gnarled limb.

Steven and Andrew broke into applause.

Gunner turned and grinned down at them. He bowed from the waist with elaborate panache. "And my next trick—"

"Gunner!" The blood rushed to Quenby's head as rage poured through her in a scarlet tide. "You get down here. Do you hear me? No more tricks."

He glanced down at her. "I only want to show Steven—" He broke off as he saw her face. "I'll be right down." He began shinnying down the trunk of the tree. "It wasn't really that dangerous, Quenby."

She wasn't listening. She had to get away from there before she exploded in front of Andrew and Steven. She gestured jerkily to the picnic basket on the ground. "I've brought your lunch, Andrew. I'll see you later. I have to get back to the house."

"Aren't you going to stay, Quenby?" Andrew's face was puzzled as he peered through the leaves. "I wanted to show you how much we've done on our house."

"I'll see it later." She turned away. "Enjoy your lunch." She found she was running, streaking through the woods as if she were pursued by demons. Damn that idiot! How did he dare do this to her?

"Quenby!" Gunner shouted.

She paid no attention. She broke out of the woods and started to run across the meadow.

"Stop!"

Why did he want her to stop? Maybe he wanted her to watch him try to break his neck again.

"Quenby, you're acting crazy. There's no reason for you to be this upset." His voice was breathless as he ran after her. "Let me explain."

The soles of her tennis shoes thudded on the wooden planking of the bridge, and then she was streaking up the steps of the back porch.

"Quenby, love," Gunner's hand fell on her shoulder even as she threw open the screen door. "You have to listen to me."

"The hell I do." She tore away from him and ran into the kitchen. "Leave me alone. Go fall off a mountain or kill yourself showing off like the idiot you are. I don't care!" She couldn't hold the tears back any longer, and she averted her face as she hurried from the kitchen and down the hall.

"Will you stop running away from me?" Gunner's voice held exasperation as well as tenderness. "I'm trying to apologize. I didn't mean to scare you. I just didn't think."

"You never do." She started up the stairs.

"It wasn't as dangerous as it appeared. I knew what I was doing. I once knew an acrobat who worked for Ringling Brothers and she taught me a few things."

"I'll bet she did."

"You're jealous." He caught up with her on the landing, grasped her by the shoulders and spun her around to face him. His grin faded as he saw her tear-streaked face and he drew her gently into his arms, cradling her with enormous tenderness. "And I'm a complete bastard for doing this to you." His head lowered and his lips feathered first one lid and then the other. "Forgive me?"

"No."

"Please?" He shifted his hands from her shoulders to cradle her cheeks in his palms. "I'll give you a present. Anything you want in the world."

"I don't want a present."

"Then you can give me one. I like presents." His lips lowered slowly toward her own. "Kiss me, Quenby."

"Why should I? I'm furious with you."

"Because I want it so much I feel as if I'm dying." He was only a breath away. "It hurts me when you're angry with me. Do you want me to show you how I'm hurting?"

"I'm hurting too."

"I know."

He smelled of soap, maple leaves, and sunlight, and the heat emitting from his body was wrapping her in a seductive spell. Her breasts were lifting and falling with every breath as that heat ignited a trembling deep within her.

"Let's help each other, love," he said. Then his

lips touched hers, not moving, not initiating, waiting.

She gave a broken little cry deep in her throat. "Gunner . . ." Her arms slid around his shoulders and she hugged him fiercely. What if she had lost him? "I think I hate you," she said huskily.

"No, you don't." He was pressing hot, urgent kisses on her cheeks and throat. "You love me. That's what this is all about. That's why you're so angry with me." His body was hardening against her and the realization sent a wild primitive thrill through her. "You know that, Quenby."

She did know it, and the knowledge was tearing her apart.

His fingers were rapidly unbuttoning her short-sleeved blouse. "It will be easier when you stop fighting it." He slipped the blouse from her shoulders and it fell to the hooked rug covering the landing. "I may not be your idea of a dream man, but I'm not so bad." He unfastened the front catch of her bra. "And no one could love you more than I do."

His lips lowered to caress the hollow of her throat, and the cadence of her heart suddenly doubled. How had they come to this point? Quenby wondered dazedly. Her emotional upheaval had ripped aside every barrier she had raised against him and left her raw and in a fever of wanting. She tried to hold on to some fragment of circumspection. "We shouldn't do this here. What if Andrew—"

"Judd is watching them and Andrew and Steven are so engrossed with their treehouse, we'll be lucky to get them in before dark."

He slowly pushed the bra aside to reveal her breasts. His breath came out in an explosive little burst and his gaze became hot, intense, as he looked at her. "And I think we'll be as busy as they are until dark." The bra joined her blouse on the landing.

Quenby, too, was beginning to think that they would be. She was experiencing an ache between her thighs and her entire body was trembling. She had never known such mindless hunger. "We should go to my room."

"Soon." His head was bending toward one of the pink crests crowning her breasts. "Sometimes it's better . . ." His voice trailed off as his mouth enveloped her nipple.

She moaned softly as she closed her eyes, and her fingers buried themselves in the crisp thickness of his pale gold hair. He was drawing strongly, his tongue teasing even while he suckled with erotic fierceness. She was vaguely conscious of his fingers on the buttons of her shorts, but she couldn't help him. She couldn't move. Every muscle was tense, straining to give more to him. She could feel his heat, his readiness of him. His lips left her and she heard the harshness of his breathing before he enveloped her other nipple with his mouth.

The shorts and the bikini panties were sliding down her legs and she stepped out of them without thinking, conscious only of Gunner, heat, and hunger.

Gunner lifted his head. "I can't wait," he muttered. "I have to get inside you, love." A flush colored his cheekbones, and his eyes were glittering brilliantly in his taut face. He pulled off his sweatshirt. "You want to make love, don't you, Quenby? Lord, I don't know if I can stop if you—"

"Yes, yes," she murmured. She stepped closer, her breasts pressing against the triangle of springy hair on his chest. She shuddered as she felt the thatch brush against her engorged nipples. "Oh, yes, I want you, Gunner."

His big hands cupped her buttocks, squeezing and releasing as he buried his lips in the curve of her throat. "I love you. You know that, don't you? It's not just sex." He laughed shakily. "Though that's all I can think of right now." He drew her down on her knees on the carpet of the landing and carefully brought her into the concave hollow of his hips until she was pressed against the iron-hard length outlined beneath his jeans.

"Me too." She inhaled sharply as he began to rotate her against his arousal. Her hands clutched desperately at his shoulders. "I've never felt this way before. I think I'm about to melt."

"Good." His fingers fumbled with the zipper of his jeans, and his manhood suddenly sprang free, its warmth sending a shock through her as it nuzzled against her womanhood. "I want to feel you melt around me." He sat back on his heels and drew her slowly forward, penetrating her with one smooth thrust.

"Gunner!" Her throat arched as she threw back her head, her nails digging into his shoulders.

He slowly slid her down, forcing her to take more of him. "Am I hurting you?"

"No." Fullness, fire, hunger.

He arranged her legs around him. "You're so tight, you fit me so well. I love it." His chest was moving rapidly with the harshness of his breathing. He flexed within her and laughed softly as he felt the little shiver than ran through her. "Do you love it?"

"Yes . . ." She unconsciously clenched around him, wanting to take more.

He groaned, "Do that again."

"No . . . please . . ." She buried her face in his shoulder. The rough denim of his jeans chafed against her soft inner thighs and it was wildly erotic. She was burning, her breasts heavy and ripe against him. "I can't stand it. Move, Gunner . . ."

His lips brushed her temple. "It will be fine, love." His hands cupped her hips and he began moving her, lifting, igniting a fiery rhythm that shook her to the foundations of her being. "Let me do everything for you."

She could do nothing else. She felt as if she were bound by electric cords to him and could respond only as he wished her to respond. She bit her lower lip as sensation after sensation flowed through her in a searing tide.

"Soon." The word was a hoarse gasp against her ear. "I can't . . . It has to be soon, Quenby."

"I know." Had she spoken or just thought she had? She was mindless, her body conscious of only one purpose, one motion, one tension. Her blood was exploding, throbbing through every vein, and she knew this agonizing pleasure was too intense to last much longer. If it went on much longer, she would shatter.

"Now!" The rhythm escalated into almost brutal fierceness that robbed her of breath and drove her into a frenzied search for completion. She was sobbing, trembling, on fire.

She heard him give a low groan as he plunged to unbelievable depths.

Then she *did* shatter, splintering into a glittering glory of sensation. She collapsed against him, feeling as if her muscles had turned to water. She couldn't get her breath. Her eyes closed as everything spun dizzily around her.

She was dimly conscious of Gunner lifting her off him, lying her down on the carpet of the landing, but she couldn't seem to force her lids to open. She felt him moving and wondered hazily how he had the energy when she was unable to wriggle even her little finger at the moment. He was doing something with her feet . . .

She finally managed to open her eyes. "What are you doing?"

"Taking off your tennis shoes." He had stripped off his clothes, she noticed in surprise and was sleekly, beautifully, naked. He bundled up both his clothes and his own garments. "*Now* we can go to bed, love."

"We can?" She gazed at him in bemusement. "I don't think I can move."

"I'll help you." Holding their clothes in one arm, he took her hand and pulled her to her feet. He smiled down at her, his gaze moving possessively over her lush curves. "Lord, you're wonderful." His arm slid around her waist as he propelled her gently up the stairs. "But I knew you would be." His warm lips brushed her cheek.

Her eyes twinkled with sudden amusement. "I hope you found me 'comfortable.' "

He grimaced. "You're not going to let me forget that, are you? No, my love, you were *not* comfortable. You drove me to the brink of insanity. You're the sexiest lady I've ever met, and I can't wait to let you drive me crazy again."

They were at the top of the stairs, and Quenby looked back at the landing with disbelief. It seemed impossible that they were both standing there naked, in the middle of the afternoon, after indulging in a bout of lovemaking so wild that it had caused her to behave in a fashion totally foreign to her. "I think I'm the one who has gone crazy. I don't believe I've ever been this impetuous. Are you always so impatient?"

"No." He was silent as they covered the short distance to her room. It wasn't until the door closed behind them that he spoke again. "I was crazy for you." He dropped the clothes on the floor and propelled her toward the bed. "I'm still crazy for you." He pulled her down on the bed and into his arms. "But there was another reason I didn't want to wait until we got upstairs."

"What reason?"

"I was scared." His voice was low. "I was afraid you'd change your mind before I could show you how good it was going to be for us." His hands were running over her lightly, teasingly, and she was beginning to feel the same hot stirring she had known before. "I know you think I'm some kind of freak, but I thought if you knew I could satisfy you . . ." He was suddenly over her, parting her thighs, readying her as he was already readied.

His expression was almost fierce as he gazed down at her. "And I *did* satisfy you. I'll always be able to satisfy you. It will only get better." He slid slowly within her, filling her with his manhood.

Freak. He had referred to himself like that before, she remembered hazily. She must tell him she didn't . . .

Then both memory and thought vanished as he began to move within her.

The rays of the setting sun poured through the leaded glass windows, casting a mellow pinkish glow over the room. Such a beautiful light, Quenby thought dreamily, and its tranquility exactly fitted her mood. No one could be more mellow than she felt at the moment.

"Did you love him?" Gunner's voice was low and muffled against her shoulder. "LaCroix, I mean."

Quenby looked down at him, but his expression was hidden from her. "This is a fine time to ask. You've been telling me ever since we met that I didn't love him."

"Well, did you?"

Quenby hesitated. "No." It was true, she realized suddenly. The emotion she had felt for Raoul was minuscule in comparison to what she felt for Gunner. "I thought I was very sophisticated when I met Raoul." She shook her head. "But I was only a hayseed from Minnesota. I didn't realize that when a man told a woman he loved her, it didn't necessarily mean forever. Raoul had an altogether different set of values from mine, but I suppose I was mesmerized by him. It's not surprising when I think about it. He was a count, charming, terribly good-looking and he—"

"That's enough," Gunner interrupted gruffly. "I wanted reassurance, not a catalogue of the bastard's attractions."

"Reassurance?" Quenby asked. "You?"

"Maybe I'm not as confident as I pretend. I'm jealous as hell, you know."

"No, I didn't know." She was beginning to realize there were a good many facets to Gunner's character that still remained a mystery to her. "I would think having superior intelligence and talents that aren't possessed by anyone but a select few would give you a great deal of confidence. Why should you worry about a man like Raoul?"

"Because he's not a—" He broke off and suddenly raised himself on one elbow to look down at her, frowning moodily. "I don't want to talk about him anymore. It was a mistake. I don't want to think of anything but us." He glanced away from her. "When are you going to marry me?"

She became still. "What?"

"I know you're not sure you love me yet." There was a note of little-boy defiance in his voice. "But you have to admit that we're fantastic in bed together and I'd be damned good to you. I have plenty of money and I'll buy you anything you want. You'd have to live in our compound outside Marasef, but it's a really pretty place and I think you'd like Elizabeth and Jon."

"Why would we have to live in Marasef?" She had been jarred from the languid sensual haze, and a strange panic was coursing through her. It was all happening too fast.

"It wouldn't be safe for you anywhere else. That's why we moved to Sedikhan when Alex Ben Raschid offered us protection and a place to work. There are groups, even governments that would like to use us for their own ends. In the wrong hands we'd be a hell of a weapon." He frowned. "There will be times when I'll be forced to leave you, and I'd want to be sure you were protected."

She felt a chill, as if touched by a cool breeze. "Of course. You told me you were a troubleshooter." She pushed him away and sat up. "You'd be very good at a job like that." She swung her legs to the floor and stood up. "I can't think of anyone who's better qualified by inclination."

Gunner's eyes narrowed on her face. "What do you mean?"

"Danger." Her words were jerky. "You're hooked on it. You said your precious Clanad stays in Sedikhan because it's safer, but not Gunner Nilsen. He wanders all over the face of the earth risking his neck and—"

"It's my job, Quenby."

"The hell it is." She turned on her heel. "Not the way you do it."

"Come back to bed. We can't solve anything if you run away."

"I'm not running away." She paused at the bathroom door to look back at him. "I'm just doing my job. It's time Andrew and Steven came out of those blasted woods and had their dinner. I'm going to shower and then go after them."

"I'll do—"

"No!" She cut him short with a fierceness that startled him. "I get a great deal of satisfaction out of doing my job. It's not thrilling, I don't walk any tightropes between life and death. But then, most people don't have to do that to enjoy their work."

"You're angry. Is it genuine or a defense mechanism to avoid answering me? Don't you want to marry me, Quenby?"

"You're damn right it's genuine. I've just gotten over one relationship that tore me apart and you want me to jump into another that has more potential problems than most women would dream of trying to solve."

"But then, you're a woman who enjoys a challenge, love."

"Not one like this." She was utterly drained and she could feel the beginnings of a throbbing headache. "I'm not going to let you rush me into marriage, Gunner."

A flicker of disappointment shadowed his face before he forced a smile. "I guess I didn't really think you'd let me bulldoze you at this stage of the game, but I thought I'd give it a try. It won't be so bad if you let me rush you into bed every night." Then, as he saw her expression, he stiffened. "Not that either?"

She shook her head. "I need to think and you're—" She moistened her lips with her tongue. "I mean, you're very powerful sexually, Gunner. I'm not sure I wouldn't be influenced by that sexuality."

He smiled wistfully. "I'm counting on it."

"Oh, Gunner . . ." She stood looking at him, filled with exasperation, tenderness, and despair. "I just want to be sensible. This is a very important decision for both of us, one I can't make based on sex alone. You wouldn't want me to do that, would you?"

"Yes. I'll take you anyway I can get you, and work out the rest of the details later."

"Well, I can't make a decision that haphazardly. It's not my nature to be impulsive." She frowned. "Which should prove to you how far apart we are. We don't even think alike."

"We don't have to think alike." He suddenly smiled at her with a brilliance that caused a warm radiance to flower within her. "It's more interesting like this and it doesn't matter as long as we're *valon*."

"Gunner, what if—"

"I'll shower in my own bathroom." He hopped out of bed and began to gather the clothes he had dropped on the floor when he had first entered the room. "Then I'll start dinner while you go fetch Andrew and Steven. How about steak and salad? That should be quick."

"Fine." She was still frowning at him. "I don't

think you're taking me seriously. I mean it, you know."

"I always take you seriously." He turned at the door, his eyes twinkling. "And I'll try to be patient about the marriage." He opened the door. "But you can't expect to have it all your own way, love. Sex is a different matter entirely."

Seven

"Come on." Gunner grabbed her by the hand and pulled her down the stairs. "I've been waiting for you. Is Andrew asleep?"

She nodded, trying to keep up with his long strides as he half-pulled, half-carried her down the hall. "He and Steven played so hard today, he dropped off almost immediately. Where are we going? Is something wrong?"

"Nope." He pulled her through the kitchen and out on the back porch. "Not a thing in the world. It's just time for *us* to play now."

"Gunner, I told you last night—"

"And wasn't I wonderfully understanding and forebearing?" He grinned over his shoulder as he pulled her down the porch steps. "I didn't come to your room last night, and today I've been so discreet, I think I should qualify for sainthood."

"Why do I feel that your discretion is now a thing of the past?" she asked warily as Gunner guided her toward the stream.

"Well, I thought about it and decided I'd be doing you a disservice if I let you run the show. You need someone to ripple your quiet, placid waters." He gestured toward the paddle wheel several yards from where they were standing. "Like that paddle wheel. Now, this is a pretty little stream, but it becomes interesting only when the paddles dip into the water and churn it up a little." He smiled down at her in the moonlight, his face alive with sensuality and wicked mischief. "Like I'm going to churn you, Quenby."

Quenby experienced a melting heat between her thighs as she looked at him. His hair was shimmering like the moonlight itself, and there was a tension about his slim body that oozed sexuality. So much for her good sense and firm resistance, she thought. All the man had to do was to smile at her and the memories of those hours of passion yesterday were making her tremble with anticipation. She made an effort to keep her voice calm, but even to herself she sounded breathless. "And what if I don't want to be 'churned'?"

"Then I'll let the stream go its own way, flowing smooth and serene." His voice lowered to a seductive whisper. "And unutterably bored, love." His fingers were quickly unbuttoning her blouse. "But you really should let the paddle wheel do its work. You'll find it much more stimulating." He undid her bra and pushed it and the blouse off her shoulders to fall to the bank of the stream. "You were never meant to meander along without any surprises to challenge you." He paused, looking down at her intently. "Did you think about me last night while you were alone in your bed?"

"Yes." Her answer was only a level above a whisper. She had lain in bed aching, burning with a hunger as intense as if she had never had him, as if it were all ahead of her. "I wanted you."

"Did I ever tell you how much I love that honesty of yours? It's a constant delight to me." He stepped back and looked at her, his gaze lingering on her engorged breasts. "You want me now." He reached out to tenderly cup one breast in his hand. His palm was warm, hard in spite of its gentleness, and a shudder ran through her. "Why didn't you come to me?" He squeezed gently, watching her nipple flower and harden into prominence. "I was waiting. I'll always be waiting."

She looked down, and a ripple of heat went through her as she saw his big, tanned hand against the fairness of her flesh. Her breasts were rising and falling with every breath, and his hand was an erotic weight upon them. She couldn't think. What had he asked her? "I was trying to be . . . sensible."

His other hand moved up to gently massage the hard crest of her nipple. She bit her lower lip to keep from crying out as a tingling zinged from her breast to the center of her womanhood. "Pleasure is immensely sensible. Don't you agree?"

"I do right now."

He slowly shook his head, a smile curving his lips. "You're qualifying again, but I'll take what I can get. Undress, love."

"Here? Do you have something against bedrooms?"

"That's one of the advantages of being out in the country—there's no one around to interfere." Then, as she opened her lips to protest again, he added, "And don't worry about Andrew. You always open his window that overlooks the paddle wheel and we'll hear him if he calls out." He was quickly stripping, and she found herself gazing at him instead of undressing herself.

The line of his buttocks was truly magnificent. Well-muscled, tense and taut, and his powerful thighs were dusted with hair as golden as the hair on his head. He stood there, naked, and she wanted to look at him forever.

He laughed softly. "You're slow. Need some help? It would be my pleasure."

"No." She suddenly felt a wild exhilaration surge through her, as giddy as it was unexpected. She kicked off her tennis shoes and started to unbutton her shorts. "I think it's time I participated a little more actively. I'm tired of being passive."

He looked surprised. "I didn't notice any undue passivity. I thought you were very cooperative."

"Did you?" She tossed back her hair, loving the feel of it on her bare shoulders. "But I don't want to cooperate. I want to initiate." She was naked now and stepped closer, brushing her lips against his cheek and then closer still until her nipples pressed against his chest. "Like this."

He gasped, and she felt a shudder vibrate through his every muscle.

Her hand reached out and curved around his manhood. "And this."

He groaned deep in his throat as he stood still, waiting.

"And *this*." Her hand tightened and then released him, and she laughed as she whirled away from him.

"Quenby, for heaven's sake, what—"

She jumped from the bank into the stream. The icy water was flowing silk on her hot flesh. "Come on, Gunner, it feels wonderful."

"I didn't have a swim in mind," Gunner said as he stepped into the stream. "But if the lady desires . . ."

"Oh, the lady desires." She stood on tiptoe in the shallow stream, the water barely reaching her chin. She moved closer and rubbed against Gunner's hard body with teasing sensuality. "Many things."

He gazed down at her, his eyes glittering in the moonlight. "You know you're driving me crazy and you're enjoying the hell out of it. I believe I've just discovered a new Quenby Swensen." He caught her hand and led her back to the bank, lowering her onto the nest of their clothing. He pressed her against his rigid arousal. "I like Quenby the seductress." He lowered his head and found her lips parted, waiting. His tongue entered, explored, and he felt her heart leap and then accelerate wildly in response. He lifted his head and undulated his lower body against hers. "So seduce me already."

Quenby felt weak. The muscles of her belly clenched and relaxed and clenched again as he moved against her. "I think I prefer it be a mutual seduction," she said faintly as her hands clung tightly to his shoulders. "I don't think I have the aggressiveness for—" She broke off as she felt him rub her slowly. She arched against him with a low cry.

"I don't think so either." He smiled, watching her face, then rose, lifting her with him and setting her on her feet. "You're a very hot lady and that's seduction enough," he said as he mounted her on himself with one smooth stroke.

He threw back his head, his eyes closed in an agony of pleasure. "Help me," he gasped. "Your legs . . ."

Her legs went around his hips, clasping him desperately as his palms cupped her buttocks and began to move her. So full . . .

She bit her lip to keep from moaning as the searing pleasure speared through her in a rhythm that was wildly sensual.

The hard paddles slapping the smooth water next to them. Gunner's hardness striking within her. All one. Hardness against smoothness. The turbulence grew, spread, until it was so intense she wasn't certain she'd be able to stand it. Her nails dug into his back in a frenzy of hunger. "Gunner."

"Give me *more*." His teeth were clenched as he drove harder, deeper. "I need—"

There was no more to give him, but then, no more was needed as the turbulence mounted and then exploded into a wild shower of excitement.

They were panting, clutching each other with desperate strength. "I think I'd better let you down," Gunner said, and then promptly tightened his arms around her. "Damn, I want to keep you like this for the next fifty years or so. How about it?"

"I'm game," she whispered. She didn't want to leave him either. He felt so good, so part of her, so *right*. "Do you think we could arrange something?"

"I doubt it." He kissed her long and sweetly. "Maybe I could put the Clanad to work on it. Every single one of them is into problem-solving." He slowly, reluctantly, lifted her off him and set her back on her feet. "That was pretty fantastic for an opener."

Her knees were so weak she was still clinging to him to keep herself upright. "Opener? I'm about to fall to pieces."

"I wouldn't want that to happen. I'm very fond of you just as you are." He kissed her quick and hard. "I guess I'll have to give you a chance to recover." He settled her on their clothing and said, "Stay here. I'll be right back." He started for the house at a trot and called over his shoulder. "Now, don't start thinking again, for heaven's sake. Just operate on instinct, okay?"

The screen door slammed behind him.

Quenby gazed bemusedly at the screen door and came close to laughing aloud. She certainly hadn't been thinking very clearly or reasonably so far tonight. She had let Gunner seduce her and tempt her into doing whatever he wanted.

No, that wasn't true. Gunner may have been the aggressor, but she had yielded only because she had wanted to yield. Her body had been hungry for him and she had given it exactly what it wanted: Gunner.

She was feeling delightfully languid, her body still flushed with pleasure. Yet, curiously, she felt no repleteness as she sat there. The warm breeze touching her damp body was like a caress, and she felt again the stirring of that wild exhilaration. What was happening to her?

The screen door slammed again and Quenby watched Gunner hurrying toward her, his arms holding a small mountain of white terry cloth, two towels and both their robes. He dropped the robes and one of the towels and began to dry her quickly and efficiently with the other towel.

"Are you all right?" he asked quietly.

"Fine." The rough toweling was as sensual as the breeze on her skin as she stood silently letting him do as he wished with her. "That feels good."

"Does it?" He smiled, and his hand slowed and began rubbing in circles. "I like it too." He finally dropped the towel and picked up her terry robe, holding it for her to slip into. He tied the belt and then patted her affectionately on the fanny. "Run along and wait for me on the porch swing. I'll be right with you as soon as I dry off."

The porch swing. A faint smile curved her lips. "Are we going to do some old-fashioned spooning?"

He chuckled as he began to run the towel over his chest. "Spooning, but definitely not old-fashioned."

A frisson of excitement trembled through her. She turned and walked quickly toward the porch.

He joined her in a few moments and dropped down next to her on the swing. He was wearing the white terry robe just like her own.

"We must look like Barbie and Ken." She laughed. "Unisex."

"Never." He slid to the end of the wooden swing and pulled her down so that she was lying on his lap cradled in his arms. "The idea revolts me. I always say, *vive la différence*." He pulled open her robe and looked down at her full breasts. "I love your breasts." He began playing, squeezing, not trying to arouse, just enjoying the textures of her. He set the swing to gliding back and forth. "I like this too. You feel . . . mine."

She felt that possession with more force now than when she had been joined to him. There was something excruciatingly intimate about lying here with his hands taking liberties with her body in this casual fashion. He tugged teasingly at her nipple. "These are so pretty. Elizabeth nursed Andrew when he was born. Would you like to nurse our child?"

A tingle of shock went through her. "What?"

He felt her stiffen and his eyes shifted from her breasts to her face. "You don't like the idea?"

"I've always thought I would breastfeed my children," she said. "It's considered better psychologically and nutritionally for an infant but . . ."

He became still. "Maybe you don't like the idea of having *my* baby? He'd probably turn out like Andrew, you know. He'd be the same or stronger than any member of the Clanad. I can't promise you a nice, normal, suburban baby."

"It's not that."

His lips tightened. "Then what is it?"

"Andrew is a wonderful child, absolutely lovable. I'd be pretty stupid not to want a child like him just because he has rather unusual gifts. But you're *pushing* me again, dammit. We've known each other for only a few days and all of a sudden you're talking about me having your baby."

His tense muscles relaxed, and he smiled down at her. "Is that all?" He resumed his toying with her nipple. "But it's not for me, Quenby. I've always loved kids, but I could wait for a year or two for my own. I'd probably prefer to have you to myself for a while." His smile faded as he gazed down at her with glowing tenderness. His face had held this same loving radiance when he had looked down at Andrew as he had rocked him to sleep, she remembered with poignancy. "It's for *you.* You're the type of woman who needs a child to complete her, love. Even if I hadn't realized that for myself, the report the Clanad did on you would have told me. You need a child of your own. I want to give you that child, Quenby." He lifted her higher and began to suck at her breast. "Will you let me do that, love?" Each word was a warm, sensual kiss with tongue and lips. His hand brushed aside the robe and his palm began to rub slowly over her belly. "I want to give you everything you want."

She was beginning to feel a primitive stirring as his words struck a chord deep within her. Gunner's child. A child with white-gold hair and a smile that shimmered with gentleness and love. She *wanted* that child. "Gunner."

His hand stilled on her abdomen as if he could already sense life. "He'll be right here. I'll feel him stirring, moving." His eyes held her own. "I think I would be a good father, Quenby."

He'd be a wonderful father, she thought, her throat tightening. He'd be strong, yet as gentle and sensitive to a child's needs as he was to her own. Waves of emotion shivered through her, and she suddenly felt the tears brim and roll down her cheeks.

"Hey!" He touched her damp cheek with gentle fingers. "You're not supposed to do this. We don't have to have a baby right away. I only wanted to let you know I wanted it too. We'll wait as long as you want."

She buried her head in the rough terry cloth covering his chest.

Gunner's hand stroked her hair. "Quenby . . ."

"I'm all right," she said huskily. "Nothing's wrong. I'm just being stupid."

He shook his head. "We'll talk about this another time. I didn't realize you'd react like this." He lifted her chin on the curve of his finger to look down into her eyes. "I guess I don't know you as well as I thought I did."

She smiled shakily. "Well enough to suggest I become the mother of your child."

"But that was natural, that's all a part of—"

"*Valon,*" she finished for him. "Well, I'm not exactly accustomed to thinking in those terms. You'll have to give me more time."

"No problem. Now that we've discussed this, we can wait for the right time for you." His eyes were suddenly glinting with mischief. "And now I propose a distraction to end the evening on a positive note."

"Distraction?"

He was moving her so that she was astride him, parting her robe and his own. The shock of his manhood against her made her inhale sharply.

He laughed softly. "Why don't I show you just how erotic porch-swing spooning can be?"

And he proceeded to demonstrate.

It was close to three in the morning when Gunner and Quenby slowly mounted the steps to the second floor.

His arm was around her waist in loving possession, and that was how she felt: Loved and possessed. The realization sent a vague, unaccountable sense of uneasiness through her.

Gunner stopped at the head of the stairs to look gravely down at her. His voice was low. "I'd like to sleep with you, but I don't think you're ready for that yet. I've been crowding you too much as it is." His fingertips touched her cheek. "But I had to have you tonight, love. We were both hurting and we needed it. And I don't promise I won't do it again the next time it gets to be too much for us."

She gazed at him uncertainly. She had been expecting him to move forward with aggression and boldness now that she had yielded so much.

"Don't look at me like that," he said wistfully. "I'm trying to remember that we'll have all our lives to lie together and hold each other. I know you're unsure, but it would be so easy." His fingertips feathered her lips. "Go to bed. I'll see you in the morning."

"Aren't you going to bed?"

He shook his head. "I'm going to sit with Andrew awhile."

Her eyes widened in alarm. "Why? He's not having a nightmare or we would have heard him cry out."

"I just want to sit and look at him." He smiled. "Sometimes it's pretty nice just to be near someone you love, and I'll be on hand if he does need me later."

Those caretaking instincts again, she thought as a glowing tenderness invaded her. Oh, dear, she wished he wouldn't do things like this. It was causing her love for him to grow in leaps and bounds, sweeping reason and her usual discretion away in its wake. "You should get your rest."

"Later." He tidied the lapels and tightened the belt of her robe as if she were a child Andrew's age. "Next time I want you to tell me you love me, Quenby. I need to know that." His lips twisted ruefully. "Though I can't say that omission will stop me from trying to seduce you if you're too slow about it." He turned toward Andrew's door. "I'm not a very patient man, and I love you, Quenby."

Quenby gazed at the panels for a long time after he had closed the door behind him. She felt lonely, curiously hollow inside. All she would have to say were three words and she would be swept into a world where loneliness would never exist for her again. Why couldn't she say those words?

She sighed and started down the hall to her own room. Her experience with Raoul, her fear of the daredevil qualities that seemed an integral part of Gunner's character, the brevity of their whirlwind relationship. Her hesitation could be for any or all of those reasons, but dissecting them wouldn't make her forget the wistfulness of Gunner's face before he had left her.

And it wouldn't make the bed she was going to any less lonely.

"Steven is going to like this." Andrew taped a big red bow on the corner of the dark-blue package and then moved the gift to the center of his bed to gaze at it admiringly. "You're right, Quenby. It's much better than a big book."

"Well, he'd better like the book too," Quenby said. "That's what I'm giving him and Gunner went into town this morning and bought him a telescope."

"He did?" Andrew's small face lit with delight. "It's going to be a great party. Did you get the strawberry ice cream?"

"You know I did." Quenby smiled indulgently. "All is as you commanded, my lord."

He chuckled. "I didn't mean to be bossy. It's just that Steven—"

"I know you didn't." She scooted over on the bed to hug him affectionately. He smelled so sweet from his bath and his body was warm and solid in her arms. In moments like these it was possible to believe he was no more than the adorable child she had first thought him. Yet what other five-year-old would manifest this concern and fierce protectiveness over someone like Steven? She released him reluctantly. "I have to go down to finish the table decorations. Suppose you run next door to Steven's apartment and get him. It's almost six o'clock." She glanced at the soft rain streaming against the panes of the window. "Be sure you wear your slicker."

He nodded absently, one hand caressing the flat oblong package lovingly. "Will it be okay if he opens my present last? It's sort of special." He added quickly, "Not that he won't think your presents are pretty special too."

"I think it would be a very good idea to save your present for last." Quenby stood up. "Shall I take it down to the dining room with me?"

His hand tightened on the package. "I'll do it."

She smiled understandingly. "All right. Thirty minutes. Okay? Gunner won't want his pot roast to get cold."

Andrew jumped up and ran to the closet. "We'll be here." He dragged his yellow slicker from the hanger. "I promise, Quenby."

Steven was dazed as he studied the long white cylinder of the telescope. His cheeks were flushed with excitement as he ran one callused finger over the smooth metal. "I can really see them? I can just look through there and see Venus and the stars of the Milky Way and . . ." He trailed off, his voice hoarse and uneven. "All of them?"

Gunner nodded. "Don't expect them to be right on top of you, but I think you'll be able to see them a great deal better than with the naked eye."

Steven's fingers moved from the telescope to touch the beautifully illustrated book on the table in front of him. "All of them."

There was a lump in Quenby's throat as she looked at him. Steven was dressed in the same kind of rough work clothes he had worn when she had first met him, but his graying hair was slicked back and carefully combed and she could visualize his earnest face as he must have stood before the mirror preparing himself for his party. Now that face was glowing like a star itself.

"My present now." Andrew pushed the flat package toward him. "Open it, Steven."

Steven tore off the navy-blue wrapping, careful to save the red satin bow. He opened the cardboard folder and gazed at the colorful, beautifully inscribed certificate with puzzled eyes. "Thank you, Andrew, it's really pretty."

Andrew's face fell in disappointment. "Don't you like it?"

"Sure I like it. It's nice. All those swirly colors . . ."

Then Andrew understood. He slipped out of his seat and came to stand by Steven's chair. "Let me help you read it. This fancy printing is kind of hard if you aren't used to it." One arm slipped protectively around Steven's broad shoulders as Andrew's index finger moved over the words of the parchment. "It says that this document certifies that the name of the star Vela Ra eight h fifty-four m four-hundred-seventy-five d-fifty-five nineteen has been officially changed to Steven Blount and has been so registered in the International Star Registry in Geneva, Switzerland." He quickly unfolded the map beneath the certificate and pointed to the star circled in red. "There it is, Steven. That's *your* star. The Steven Blount Star."

Steven was sitting frozen, his hazel eyes glittering as he stared blindly down at the map. "I've got a star of my own?" He whispered. "You named a star for me?"

Andrew's gaze drank in every nuance of Steven's emotions. "You've got a star of your own. Do you like it?"

Steven nodded jerkily. "Oh, yes, Andrew." His voice was so low, it could scarcely be heard. "It's a forever present, isn't it? For the rest of my life I can look up and know there's something of mine out there, a star with my name on it."

Quenby couldn't bear any more. She hurriedly pushed her chair back and jumped to her feet. "I have to put the candles on the cake. I'll be right back."

Her hands were trembling as she set the red and white striped candles in the chocolate icing of the cake, and she was forced to stop every now and then to wipe her eyes.

"Need any help?" Gunner was standing beside her. He picked up the matchbook on the counter, struck a match, and began to light the candles. "Though I don't know if either one of them will be interested in the cake. They're too busy looking at the map and planning their next night of stargazing. It's too bad it's raining tonight. Steven is wild to use his new telescope to try to sight his star."

"Tomorrow is supposed to be clear." Quenby's voice was shaking as she carefully avoided his eyes. "And Steven has to blow out the candles and make a wish. It's part of the tradition. I'll just take the cake in."

Gunner blew out the match and dropped it on the counter. "I'll do it." He lifted her chin and smiled at her. "And don't start arguing with me about taking over your duties. The boys wouldn't understand why you're crying when they're both so happy." He kissed her lightly. "Now, wash your face and come in with a big smile to watch the ceremony. I think Steven has already gotten his wish."

"Andrew wanted to give him something beautiful."

"And you helped him to do it. Where did you find out about the star registry?"

"I read about it somewhere. I'm so glad it worked out. We all need something beautiful in our lives."

Gunner picked up the tray with the birthday cake blazing with candles and turned toward the door. "That's what I've been trying to convince you for the last two days." His tone was bland. "And after I get Andrew and Steven settled before the TV set with a triple-header of Star Wars films in the video recorder, I intend to redouble my efforts. Tonight you're going to tell me you love me, Quenby. After this softening-up, you're bound to be putty in my hands."

Gunner was in the parlor setting up the video

recorder when the bell of the front door chimed softly.

The sound sent a faint ripple of shock through Quenby. She had become so accustomed to the comfortable isolation of Mill Cottage that even the thought of an intrusion was abrasive. The bell chimed again. Obviously Gunner was involved with Andrew and Steven and hadn't heard it. She closed the dishwasher, set it on the regular cycle, and left the kitchen.

She swung open the dutch door to reveal a tall, slim man dressed for the weather in a hooded khaki poncho and rubber boots. A flashing white smile lit the darkness of his face as he pulled back his hood to reveal closely cropped black hair. "You must be Quenby. I'm Judd Walker."

Quenby felt another tingle of apprehension which she quickly smothered. There didn't have to be something wrong just because Andrew's bodyguard had decided to make himself known to her. "Gunner told me you were here to keep an eye on Andrew. I'm very glad to meet you. Won't you come in? We're having a birthday party and—" She stopped. Judd Walker's smile remained just as pleasant but he was shaking his head. "No?"

"I need to see Gunner, if you don't mind," he said. "I'll keep him only a few minutes."

"I'll go get him. At least, come in out of the rain."

Gunner was suddenly beside her. "What is it, Judd?"

"Probably nothing." Judd's polite smile faded as he met Gunner's gaze. "I was walking through the woods when I felt something."

"Which woods?"

Judd motioned to the thick shrubbery across the road. "It was only for a second but—"

Gunner's gaze followed the gesture. "Bardot?"

Quenby felt her heart lurch sickeningly.

"I don't know." Judd's expression was troubled. "I never ran across Bardot in the old days, but this was something pretty unpleasant."

Gunner laughed harshly. "I believe that would accurately describe Bardot. You were right to come straight to me." He turned, opened the door of the hall closet, and jerked his black jacket from the hanger. "I'll go with you and you can show me where—"

"You're going into those woods?" Quenby couldn't take her eyes from the shadowy stand of trees across the road. Was someone standing there watching them even now? The soft patter of rain on the leaves would mask any rustle of movement as the darkness would veil a man's presence from view. "That's crazy. If he's there, he could jump out before you even knew what happened."

"He'd signal his intention before he moved." Gunner pulled on his jacket. "Lock the doors and the windows and don't let anyone into the house while I'm gone. I'll ring the bell when I come back, but don't open the door until you know who's on the other side."

"When will you be back?"

"When I'm sure," Gunner said grimly as he joined Judd on the porch. "One way or the other."

The front door shut behind him.

Quenby stood frozen in the foyer for a moment,

trying to force the icy numbness to leave her. He was gone. Even now he would be crossing the road toward whatever lay waiting in the darkness of the woods. She wanted to tear open the door and run after him, grab him and hold on to him before he could risk himself again.

She took a half step forward and then stopped. She couldn't abandon Andrew and Steven. They were her responsibility and she must keep them safe. She drew a deep breath, her hands clenching slowly at her sides. She must do as Gunner had said and try not to think of the danger he might encounter.

She reached out and shot the bolt on the front door and then hurried down the hall toward the kitchen to lock the back door. Within five minutes she had locked all the windows and the house was secure.

Or as secure as she could make it.

Locks could be broken and windows smashed.

The thought send her scurrying back to the kitchen to load the remainder of the birthday cake, plates, and forks on the portable cart. Then, with great deliberation, she took a shiny butcher knife from the cutlery drawer and placed it on the cart instead of the cake cutter.

She wheeled the cart down the hall and into the parlor, where Steven and Andrew were sitting on the love seat; they were absorbed by the movie. "Mind if I join you? It's been a long time since I've seen *Star Wars*. I've brought us all a snack for later." She dropped down into the easy chair closest to the door, making sure the cart and the butcher knife were both in easy reach. "Has Luke met Han Solo yet?"

Gunner had been gone for more than two hours and Quenby had just put the tape of *The Empire Strikes Back* on the video recorder when the doorbell chimed.

Quenby hurried to the front door and was about to open it just as she remembered Gunner's warning. "Gunner?"

"It's me."

Relief poured through her as she unlocked the door and threw it open.

Gunner was soaked to the skin, his white-gold hair rain-darkened to pale brown, his expression grim. "Are you all right?"

"Fine." She stepped aside to let him come in and then locked the door behind him. "Why shouldn't we be? We were safe inside while you were out there—" She broke off as she realized she was ranting at him when all she wanted to do was hurl herself into his arms. Lord, she had been frightened for him. "Where's Judd?"

"I sent him ahead to contact Marta and start servicing the Learjet." He dripped a flurry of water on the braided rug as he took off his jacket. "Are the boys still in the parlor?"

She nodded. "You couldn't pry them away from those Star Wars movies."

"I'm afraid we'll have to try." Gunner started up the steps. "I'll pack a suitcase for you and Andrew, but we'll have to get Steven a complete new wardrobe when we get to Sedikhan. I don't want anyone going to his flat to pack anything. And you'll have to leave your harp here until I can arrange for someone to pick it up and send it to you."

"We're leaving now?"

He paused on the landing to look down at her. "Right away. You should arrive in Marasef tomorrow morning. Will you turn off the electricity and get Steven and Andrew into their slickers?"

"He's out there? You saw him?"

He wearily shook his head. "It was black as Hades out there. I blundered around in the dark for two solid hours, but I couldn't find a trace of him." His lips thinned. "He was there all right. I caught a fragment of static twice. One up ahead of me and then once at my rear. I was afraid he was doubling back toward the house, so I gave up and came straight back."

"It's definitely Bardot?" she whispered.

"No question about it. Which means we've got to get Andrew out of here." He didn't wait for her to answer but started up the stairs again.

Bardot was here. The realization sent a shock wave through Quenby that spurred her into action. She ran down the hall to make sure all the appliances were turned off, then ran back to the hall closet for Andrew's and Steven's slickers.

"I'm sorry, but we'll have to save the rest of this Star Wars extravaganza for another time," she said lightly as she entered the parlor. "Gunner's received an unexpected message and we have to go back to Sedikhan." She switched off the video recorder and ejected the tape. "Put on your slickers."

"Mama?" Andrew's gravelly voice was tense with concern. "Is Mama hurt or—"

"No." Of course a child as sensitive as Andrew would jump to that conclusion. "No one is hurt or sick. Your parents are fine, Andrew. It's another kind of emergency."

"I don't want to leave now."

"I'm sorry, dear, we have to go."

Andrew cast a quick glance at Steven and then jumped to his feet. "I have to see Gunner. Where is he?"

"Upstairs packing."

"I'll be right back, Steven. Don't . . ." The rest of the words were lost as he ran from the room.

Quenby gazed after him in bewilderment. It was natural for him to be disappointed but not this upset. "Put on your slicker, Steven."

"Can't I stay here until it's time for Andrew to leave?" Steven's voice was oddly muffled. "I won't be no bother."

Quenby whirled to face him. "Steven . . ."

He was sitting huddled on the love seat, clutching his telescope and his star map, his face a mask of misery. "I wanted Andrew to see my star. I wish it wasn't raining tonight."

He thought they were leaving him here, Quenby realized remorsefully, and Andrew had probably thought the same thing. She should have made herself more clear. "He'll see your star," she said softly. "We want you to come with us, Steven. Gunner says Sedikhan is a very nice place to live, and Andrew would miss you terribly. We'd all miss you. So you must come with us."

"You mean it? I can come along?" His face was radiant.

"We couldn't do without you."

"And I can take my telescope and my map and my book?" He was stuttering with excitement.

She nodded. "But nothing else. We have to hurry."

"I'll hurry." He stood up and thrust his arms into his slicker. "See, I'm ready to go."

"Yes, you're very quick."

"But I wish we could stay just one more day," he said wistfully. "I sure would like to see my star."

"Nights are usually very clear in the desert. Maybe you'll be able to see your star even better in Sedikhan."

"But if—"

"There's a bad man here who's trying to hurt Andrew," she said. "I know you won't frighten him by telling him."

He looked at her in surprise. "Andrew wouldn't be frightened."

"But it would still be better not to tell him."

"I guess so." He gazed at her earnestly. "Don't you worry, Quenby, I won't let anyone hurt Andrew."

For the first time she could see a shadow of maturity in Steven's face and it touched her strangely. It had always been Andrew who had been the protector. She squeezed his arm affectionately. "Well, we won't have to worry about that if we leave right away."

"Steven, it's okay." Andrew ran back into the room, his face alight. "You're coming with us!"

"I know that," Steven said with dignity. "But we've got to leave now. You put on your raincoat, Andrew."

Andrew frowned in puzzlement at this abrupt reversal of roles. "Sure." He reached for the yellow slicker draped over the arm of the chair. "Sure, Steven."

Steven carefully put his presents beneath the protective vinyl of his slicker. "And you sit in the back with me, Andrew."

Andrew's gaze slowly searched Steven's face. "That will be great."

"Come on." Gunner appeared in the doorway. He had changed into dry jeans and a sweatshirt but had slipped back on his black jacket. He tossed Quenby her olive green trench coat. "I've pulled the car around to the front of the house and put the suitcases in the trunk. Let's get out of here."

A few minutes later the gray Mercedes was pulling out of the curved driveway onto the road. The rain was still falling heavily and the wipers swooshed on the windshield.

"Lock your doors," Gunner said.

Quenby tried not to look at the blackness of the wood only a few yards to her right. She locked the rear door and then her own. "Is he . . . there?"

"I don't know." Gunner's hands tightened on the steering wheel. "I think so."

The muscles of her neck were knotted as Quenby kept her gaze rigidly on the road in front of them. The headlights splayed out, piercing the rain and the darkness ahead. "Why do you think he didn't show up before?" She tried to keep her voice inaudible to Steven and Andrew in the backseat.

"How do I know?" Gunner muttered. "Maybe he wanted to play cat-and-mouse. Unbalanced people are often into power."

"And you think Bardot is unbalanced?"

"From the static I caught, I'd say he's either trembling on the brink of insanity or already on the other side. He wasn't all that stable five years ago either."

Insanity. The concept frightened her. She swallowed. "Can't we go any faster?"

"Not in this rain." He cast her a sidewise glance. "Don't worry, you'll be safe once we reach the airport and that shouldn't take more than forty minutes. Tell Marta to radio Jon to meet you at Marasef Airport."

It suddenly occurred to Quenby that he had been saying "you" and not "we'" since he had come back to Mill Cottage. She had been so frightened and on edge, she had forgotten what he had told her about going "hunting." A surge of sheer terror tore through her. "You don't intend to come with us, do you?"

"Not right away."

"You're going to come back to try to find that madman."

"He's a danger to Andrew."

"He's also a danger to you," she said fiercely. "We'll be halfway across the world. He can't hurt Andrew in Sedikhan."

"This is the second time he's been a threat to us." Gunner didn't look at her. "We can't afford to let him go again."

"Gunner don't do—"

"Hush!" Gunner tensed, his gaze searching the darkness ahead. "There's something . . ."

A man was standing in the middle of the road in front of them!

A gun! The man's arm was extended and he was pointing a pistol directly at their oncoming car.

Quenby was only marginally conscious of the man's wild, glazed eyes and bulldog jowls as Gunner instinctively hit the brakes. Bardot. It had to be Bardot.

The Mercedes slid sidewise toward the man as Gunner fought desperately to regain control of the vehicle.

Bardot seemed to be impervious to any danger to himself as he strode toward the skidding car.

He was beside the car now, peering into the backseat, the muzzle of the gun pressed against the glass.

"Get down on the floor." Gunner shouted, still fighting the wheel. "Bardot, listen—"

It was too late! The glass shattered as the bullet exploded against the back window. She heard Andrew cry out. Oh, God, Andrew was shot!

Bardot's big bulk vanished from beside the car and Quenby caught a fleeting glimpse of his running figure disappearing into the woods.

"Andrew!" Gunner cried in anguish as he pulled up the lock on the back door, opened his door, and stepped out onto the pavement. "My God . . ." He jerked open the rear door to look inside.

Quenby had climbed over the seat into the rear of the car. She swallowed. Oh, Lord, she felt sick.

It wasn't Andrew who had been shot. Steven was slumped across Andrew, blood pouring from a wound on his left temple.

Andrew was sobbing, holding Steven's big body close, and rocking him in an agony of grief. "He pushed himself in front of me. He's hurt, Quenby. I think he's dying. Help him! He pushed in front of me. . . ."

Quenby could feel the helpless tears streaming down her face. Oh, God, not Steven, with his simplicity and his gentle shining. Not Steven, who had overcome his child's mind to become something more than what he was, to become . . . caretaker.

Eight

"Andrew, you can't help him," Quenby said gently. "They won't let anyone see Steven. Why won't you let me take you home to bed?"

Andrew shook his head.

Quenby's hands clenched in her lap as she forced herself to look away from Andrew's small figure huddled in the padded green plastic chair. He looked so desolate, so damned *alone*. It wasn't good for him to be here in this sterile waiting room, but every effort to get him to leave had been met with this same silent, determined resistance. Her gaze shifted to the window and she noticed numbly that the rain had finally stopped and the sky was beginning to lighten with the pearly softness of predawn. How many hours had they been here? Ten? Twelve? It had seemed forever.

"Quenby."

She looked up to see Gunner beside her holding two large glasses of orange juice in his hands. He handed her one of the glasses. "Drink it. You need the vitamins."

"Did you see the doctor?"

He nodded wearily and lowered his voice so Andrew could not hear him. "They still don't know anything for certain. It could still go either way. Marta left a message at the nurses' station for me that Jon and Elizabeth are on the way from the airport. They should be here within thirty minutes."

"You called them?"

"As soon as we got Steven into the emergency room." He smiled mirthlessly. "I knew how Andrew would react and I thought I'd better call for reenforcements. I sure as hell haven't done very well on my own."

"You did everything you could. As soon as you knew there was danger, you tried to get us away. It all happened so fast! You can't blame yourself."

"The hell I can't." There was barely leashed savagery in Gunner's tone. "Steven is lying in a hospital bed dying and Andrew is sitting over there in a near catatonic state again. This plan was all my idea and they were my responsibility. I searched until I found the one person who was sure to become Andrew's closest friend and then I almost managed to get him killed."

"Gunner . . ." There was such torment and exhaustion in Gunner's face that Quenby experienced an aching sympathy for him. Andrew and Steven weren't the only casualties of this terrible night. "Bardot was too quick—"

"But I could have stopped him," Gunner interrupted harshly. "If half my mind hadn't been occupied with keeping the car from wrecking, I could have frozen him before he pulled that trigger. What the hell is the good of having powers like this if you can't help the people you love?"

"I don't know, but it's crazy to blame yourself. This wasn't your fault."

"It was my responsibility to stop Bardot. He's still out there."

"You told me yourself that the police are scouring the woods for Bardot. They'll surely find him and he'll go to trial." She had to find a way of distracting him. "Now, will you stop chastizing yourself and see what you can do to help Andrew?" She drew a quivering breath. "He's breaking my heart. I can't get him to eat or rest."

Gunner nodded. "I'll try." He crossed the room and squatted down in front of Andrew's chair. "I brought you a glass of orange juice, Andrew."

Andrew shook his head.

"Don't say no." Gunner took Andrew's hand and folded it around the glass. "I'm not telling you that you have to eat anything right now, but this will give you the energy to get through the next few hours without collapsing. If you want to stay close to Steven, you have to take care of yourself."

Andrew's hand tightened on the glass. "He's dying, isn't he, Gunner?"

Gunner hesitated. "I've never lied to you and I'm not going to start now. We don't know. The bullet didn't pierce Steven's temple, but the angle of the shot caused the bullet to act like a heavy blow. That blow was very severe and he's gone into a deep coma. The doctors think shock may have something to do with it."

"Coma. That means he's asleep and won't wake up." Andrew's voice was curiously flat. "It's like death."

Gunner shook his head. "He may wake up at any time. We just don't know, Andrew. Some people wake up right away and some don't wake for a long time."

"But the longer he stays asleep . . ." Andrew met his gaze with the clarity and directness of a young man not a small child. "It's dangerous, isn't it?"

"Yes," Gunner said softly. "It is dangerous. The will to live has a good deal to do with survival, and when someone goes into a coma, they can't consciously fight."

"But Steven *does* want to live." Andrew said, frowning thoughtfully. "He was so happy about going to Sedikhan and seeing his star."

"Then maybe, somehow, he'll remember that and wake up," Gunner said. "We hope so."

"We ought to be able to do more than hope." Andrew lifted the glass to his lips and took a sip of the orange juice. "I'll have to think about it."

"You do that." Gunner's hand closed affectionately on his shoulder. "And after you finish that juice, don't you suppose it would be a good idea to let Quenby take you down to the cafeteria for some breakfast? You can't think clearly on an empty stomach."

"What?" Andrew was still frowning in abstraction and he obviously had to pull his attention back to Gunner. "Oh, I guess so."

Quenby breathed a sigh of relief. She had been worried that Andrew wouldn't be able to face the honesty of Gunner's words, but the boy had responded amazingly well.

Gunner was crossing the room toward her and his expression was once more taut with tension. "You'd better have breakfast too."

She nodded. "I will. How about you?"

"I don't know. I'm not—"

"How is he?" It was a breathless feminine voice and they both turned to see a tall brown-haired woman in her early thirties standing in the doorway of the waiting room.

"Elizabeth." Gunner hurried forward to press a warm kiss on the woman's smooth cheek. "Where's Jon?"

"He stopped to talk to the doctor. I wanted to see Andrew . . ." Even as she spoke she was hurrying across the room to where her son was sitting. "Hi, fella, you've had some pretty tough going, haven't you?"

"Mama?" Andrew was staring at her in disbelief. Then a radiant smile lit his face and he jumped to his feet and hurled himself at her. "I didn't know you were coming."

"Where else would I be?" Elizabeth rescued the orange juice and set it on the table beside his chair before enfolding Andrew in a fierce hug. "You okay?"

Andrew nodded, his arms holding his mother tightly. "But Steven's hurt, Mama."

"I know. But we're going to do everything we can to help him." Elizabeth gave him another hug and then released him. "Your father's talking to the doctor now."

"Quenby was just going to take Andrew down to the cafeteria to get a bite of breakfast," Gunner said quietly. "You look like you could do with a cup of coffee yourself."

"Stop mothering me, Gunner." Elizabeth wrinkled her nose at him. "I know I look like a hag, but I couldn't sleep on the plane." She turned to Quenby. "Hello, Quenby. I guess you've realized by now that I'm this young man's mother. I want to thank you for taking such good care of my son."

"I've loved doing it. Andrew's a wonderful boy."

A smile lit Elizabeth's freckled face with a special beauty. "He'll do. I've decided to keep him." She took Andrew's hand. "Now, let's go get that breakfast."

Andrew's face was suddenly shadowed by a troubled frown. "Maybe I should stay here in case Steven—"

"Suppose I stay here," Quenby interjected quickly. "Then, if you're needed, I can come and get you. You can bring me something."

Andrew's face lightened with relief. "Would you do that, Quenby? I don't like to leave Steven."

"I'll be right here," Quenby promised.

"Thank you." For a moment Elizabeth's amber eyes reflected the weariness and anxiety she was determinedly hiding from Andrew. Then she was smiling again. "We'll tell them they have to pre-

pare something really special in the way of breakfast to bring up to you." She turned to Gunner.
'Tell Jon where I am. Okay?"

Gunner nodded. "I'm sorry about all this,
Elizabeth."

"I knew you'd be suffering a kingsize guilt trip,
but no one's blaming you, Gunner," Elizabeth
said gently. "You did the best you could. We all
know that." She looked down at Andrew. "Jon and I
both believe it was just bad luck that things turned
out as they did."

A moment later Elizabeth and Andrew had left
the waiting room and were walking down the hall
toward the bank of elevators.

"I like her," Quenby said softly. "She's very
strong, isn't she?"

"She's had to be," Gunner said. "She's a hell of
a woman." He paused. "But so are you. Thanks
for being here for me, Quenby. It helped."

"Nonsense. As Andrew's mother said, 'Where
else would I be?' I was needed here and I care as
much about Steven as you and Andrew."

"I know you do." Gunner stood looking at her.
"I just wanted you to know . . ." He shook his
head. "I can't seem to think. Everything is all
jumbled in my head." He drew a deep breath and
crossed the few steps separating them. "Quenby."
He pulled her to him and kissed her with yearning tenderness. "Oh, Quenby."

Then he released her, and before she could say
a word he had left the waiting room and was
walking down the hall away from her.

She gazed after him blankly, and it was not

until the elevator doors had closed behind him that she realized he had been telling her good-bye.

He was going after Karl Bardot.

"You must be Quenby Swensen. I'm very happy to meet you at last. I'm Jon Sandell."

Quenby turned from gazing blindly out the window to watch Jon Sandell striding across the waiting room toward her.

The smile lighting his darkly bronzed face was every bit as charismatic as that of his wife, Elizabeth, and he exuded vitality and authority. "We've really imposed on your patience and understanding, haven't we? God knows we had no idea any of this would happen."

"It was my choice to stay." Quenby had to force the words through stiff lips. "I'd do it again."

Jon Sandell sighed ruefully. "Then you're a glutton for punishment. You look as if you're about to collapse. Where's Andrew and my wife?"

"The cafeteria." Quenby folded her arms across her chest. She was shaking with cold. How strange, the room was really quite warm. "Andrew seems to be much calmer."

"Good." Jon frowned. "Though there's no telling how he'll react if Steven Blount—" He broke off. "We'll cross that bridge when we come to it. Did Gunner go with them?"

"No." She lifted her gaze to meet his own. "He's gone after Karl Bardot."

Jon went still. "I guess I should have expected that."

She nodded jerkily. "It was no real surprise to me."

His eyes narrowed on her face. "No?"

"He likes it. He gets some kind of kick out of—" She stopped as her throat tightened with emotion. "I'm sorry, I'm a little upset. I don't think I'd better talk about this any longer."

"On the contrary, I think we'd do well to discuss it," he said bluntly. "There's obviously trouble brewing between you and Gunner because of this and I'd guess there are a few things you don't know about him. I should have known he wouldn't talk about his past. He even refused to go back to the psychologists after his initial therapy."

"Therapy?" Quenby asked slowly. "Why was he in therapy?"

"Guilt. Did he tell you how his parents died?"

"No."

"They were murdered by the invading army when Said Ababa marched into Garvania—very brutally murdered. Gunner was with the Clanad at the university some distance away when Said Ababa launched the invasion and couldn't make it back to the farm for nearly two days. When he finally got there, he found his mother and father hacked to death and his home burned to the ground."

Quenby's eyes were wide with shock. "How terrible."

Jon nodded grimly. "He was just a kid at the time. He nearly went crazy with grief and blamed himself. He felt he should have been there."

"But then he would have been killed too."

"He knows that on a conscious level, but you

have to understand—" Jon paused. "Gunner's parents were good people but they weren't very well educated and they clung to the old ways. It upset them very much when Gunner left the farm and went into the army, but they could accept it. However, they couldn't accept his participation in the mirandite experiment. They thought it would turn him into some kind of a freak."

Freak. Dear heaven, she thought, he had even told her he was afraid she might think of him as a freak, and she hadn't even pursued the subject. She should have questioned him, reassured him.

"After his parents were murdered, Gunner went into a deep depression." His lips thinned. "The Clanad should have tried to help him then, but we were all pretty busy at the time. Said Ababa took all of us back to run some tests and it was a wonder that we weren't all crazy by the time we escaped from the institute. Anyway, Gunner seemed to be handling his problem pretty well and we let it go. It wasn't until later that we noticed a few personality changes. He became reckless as hell and wild as the wind. But he was still Gunner and we all loved him."

"Then why didn't you help him?" Quenby asked fiercely. "He could have been killed, dammit."

"We tried. After we settled in Sedikhan we all underwent therapy to try to increase our stability." He paused. "That's when we discovered what was wrong with Gunner. He considered himself not only to blame for his parents deaths but, in some convoluted way, he had come to believe they were right about him being a freak. On occasion the guilt feelings triggered an explosive recklessness."

"But he's still like that."

He shrugged. "Gunner accepted the therapy and came to recognize his problem but he was impatient and stopped before he was fully cured. Since Gunner was stable in every other way and never endangered anyone else, we couldn't insist on him resuming therapy. It would have interfered with his rights as an individual and the Clanad has rules—"

"Rules?" Quenby's voice was trembling. "The first time I saw him, he was dodging machine-gun bullets."

"We tried to protect him as well as we could. We gave him a job that would offer him direction and surround him with the best people available," he added softly. "People who loved him."

Marta, the atypical grandmother who was meant to save Gunner from himself, Quenby thought dully. But it hadn't worked. None of it had worked. "You should have done something more."

"The Clanad's code forbids—"

Her eyes were blazing. "Damn your code. What difference does it make if you violate his rights, if it keeps him alive?" She drew a deep, measured breath, trying to smother her anger. "Do you know what Gunner is? Do you know how loving and caring he can be? He's so wonderful and you let him go his own way, risking his life as if it didn't matter."

"He matters to us," Jon said gently. "We love him, Quenby."

"Well, you have a funny way of showing it." She smiled shakily. "But then I guess I haven't been showing I love him too well myself. A few changes have got to be made."

"What do you have in mind?"

"Do you have a car here?"

He nodded. "A rental car. It's in the parking lot."

"May I borrow it?"

He reached into his pocket and handed her a key chain. "It's a maroon Buick, the license number is on the tag. Where are you going?"

"As soon as Andrew gets back I'm going after Gunner. I should never have let him leave without me. He'll probably go back to Mill Cottage first and there's a chance I can catch him there. If not, I'll go into the woods after him." Even as she spoke, the elevator doors opened and Andrew and Elizabeth stepped out. "There they are." She started for the door. "I'll check back periodically to see how Steven is doing."

"Gunner won't like this, you know. He won't want you to place yourself in danger when Bardot is still at large."

"I can't worry about what Gunner will like," Quenby said curtly. "I'll leave that to the Clanad. I'm only worried about keeping him alive."

She didn't wait for a reply but strode down the hall toward Elizabeth and Andrew.

The gray Mercedes was parked in the driveway in front of Mill Cottage.

Quenby breathed a profound sigh of relief as she pulled in next to it and got out. Gunner was there, just as she had guessed he would be. She could only hope that he hadn't yet left the house to start searching the woods.

The front door was unlocked and her hopes lifted even further. Gunner must still be there. She stood in the foyer. The old house was silent.

"Gunner?"

She glanced into the parlor. Everything was as it had been the night before. The video tapes left hurriedly stacked on top of the TV console, the cart with the birthday cake, plates, and forks still untouched. The cushions of the love seat still carried the slightest imprint of Steven's and Andrew's presence, as if they had just gotten up and walked out the door. Oh, God, she wished they had. She wished she could turn back the clock and do it all over.

Well, she couldn't reverse time and it was foolish even to think about it. She had to do what she could now to set things right.

Perhaps Gunner was upstairs showering and changing before beginning the search, she thought. With the shower running he might not have heard her. She left the parlor and started up the stairs. She could use a shower herself after staying at the hospital all night, she thought absently.

What was bothering her? There was something nagging at her, something not as it should be. She couldn't quite put her finger on it. . . .

She had reached the top of the stairs and started

down the hall toward Gunner's room when she heard it.

The creak of a rocking chair.

The only rocking chair was in Andrew's room.

She stopped and turned slowly toward Andrew's room. The door was ajar and she could hear the rocking chair moving rhythmically with a comforting sound.

"Gunner?"

No answer.

Only the steady creak of the rocking chair.

Oh, dear Lord! Panic raced through her, stopping her breath. She wanted to bolt down the stairs and out of the house, but she couldn't move.

Because she realized what had been bothering her, what had been wrong . . .

There had been no butcher knife on that cart in the parlor.

The creak of the rocking chair suddenly stopped.

Nine

"You can't run away, you know." The deep voice was silky with satisfaction. "I'd catch you before you were halfway down to the landing, and then I'd be very angry. I'm tired of being chased by those idiot policemen, and I need my rest. Why don't you be sensible and come in to see me?"

She stood frozen, staring at the door.

"I know who you are." The shrill giggle that followed the statement sounded obscenely coy. "You're that freak's woman. I imagine you're very fond of him. They seem to be very talented at performing their black magic on you sluts." The voice paused. "Don't you want to see what I've done to your lover? He's lying right here at my feet with a knife sticking out of his chest."

The butcher knife!

She wasn't conscious of moving, but she was

suddenly across the hall, throwing wide the door to Andrew's room. Her gaze flashed to the floor and then around the room. No Gunner.

"I lied," the man sitting in the rocking chair said placidly. "Good morning, My name is Karl Bardot."

"I know." She would have recognized that face anywhere. She could still see it pressed against the window of the car as he aimed the gun at Andrew.

The same gun he was pointing at her now.

"You said you had a knife," she said dully.

"Now, that wasn't a lie." He patted his jacket pocket and she saw the black handle of the butcher knife. He smiled. "Right here. I couldn't decide whether to use a gun or knife on Gunner Nilsen. I'm still not sure. What do you think?"

"You're going to try to kill him." It was a statement.

He looked at her in surprise. "Do you know how long I've waited for their return? Every week for four long years I've come back to this tainted house and watched for them. He has to die. They all have to die. I've killed the spawn and now I must rid the world of the others."

He evidently didn't know it had been Steven and not Andrew who had been shot. Dear heaven, he *was* mad. Nothing could be more clear to Quenby as she gazed at him. "They'll put you away for the rest of your life."

"That doesn't matter." He started to rock again. His thin hair was tangled, and his ragged wet jacket and trousers looked as though they'd been stolen from a scarecrow. He seemed completely unaware of any discomfort resulting from his soaked clothing and somehow that fact frightened her even more than the threats he made and the gun he held. "It must be done. I am the chosen one."

She took a deep breath. "Where's Gunner?"

"Searching for me. I saw him go into the woods and decided to let him beat the bushes for me for a while." His lips twisted. "I spent a most unpleasant night in those woods, but the fools didn't have a chance of catching me. Neither does your freak of a lover. I'm stronger than I was five years ago." He stopped rocking and got slowly to his feet. "I'm smarter too."

"I'm sure you are." She tried to make her voice placating. "But it won't do any good to hurt Gunner."

"His death will be—" He broke off. "But you'll see what his death will be." He motioned with the gun. "Suppose we go downstairs and wait for him, I'm sure he'll be back soon. He's such a clever young man. He almost caught up with me twice in the woods last night." He crossed the room until he was barely inches away. "Move!"

She turned and preceded him across the hall and down the stairs. Her mind was racing wildly, trying to find a way out.

"You'll have to die, too, you know." Bardot said in a conversational tone behind her. "Any women who traffic with them must be eliminated so they won't be able to bear more monsters."

"Andrew's *not* a monster," Quenby said fiercely. "But a filthy child-murderer like you wouldn't know that."

She felt the muzzle of the pistol press against her spine. "*Whore.* I'll—"

"Bardot!" The front door flew open and Gunner raced into the room.

"No, Gunner! He's got a gun!" Quenby instinctively threw herself backward against Bardot and they both fell to the floor of the landing.

Bardot screamed.

Quenby shuddered as the shrillness of the cry echoed in her ears. What had happened? Had he injured himself as he fell? She had never heard a cry so frantic with pain.

"Quenby." Gunner was beside her on the landing. "For God's sake, why did you do that? I wasn't sure I'd be able to stop him before he pulled the trigger." He was kneeling beside her, ignoring Bardot as if he didn't exist.

But he did exist, Quenby thought frantically, and he had a gun and a knife. "Watch out. . . . knife."

"It's all right, he doesn't matter anymore," Gunner said impatiently. "You're the one who matters. Are you hurt?"

She shook her head, dazed. "No." She looked over at Bardot.

She inhaled sharply. Bardot was lying on the floor, his gun beside him, his unblinking eyes staring straight ahead. His face was twisted into a mask of unutterable pain. "What did you do to him?"

Gunner glanced at Bardot casually. "I froze him and then I told him to hurt."

He *was* hurting. Quenby shivered as she saw the lines of suffering carved deep on the man's face. "Can't you stop the pain now? He looks so terrible."

"I could." Gunner helped her to her feet. "But I won't." In that moment his face was cruel, merciless, and she had a fleeting memory of that moment on the plane when she had thought he had resembled a berserker. "He shot Steven and would have shot you without a qualm. Let him hurt." He went to the phone on the table in the stairwell and picked up the receiver.

Quenby swallowed as she cast another glance at Bardot before she followed him. "Are you calling the police?"

He shook his head, his fingers moving swiftly on the buttons. "Judd's still at the airport. I'm going to have him pick up Bardot and take him to Sedikhan."

"What will they do to him there?"

"I hope they'll cut off the bastard's head." Gunner scowled. "But the Clanad will probably try to heal him first. They bend over backward to avoid hurting anyone not of the group. If we get lucky, the therapy won't work and they'll turn him over to Ben Raschid for punishment." His smile was cruel. "And Alex isn't known for his mercy in cases like this."

Someone picked up the phone on the other end of the line and Gunner began to speak clearly and incisively into the receiver.

• • •

Gunner watched Judd's truck disappear around the bend of the road, and then turned back to where Quenby was standing in the foyer. "That's it, it's over." He frowned. "What's wrong? You've said scarcely a word since I made that call to Judd." Then his expression softened. "Don't worry, the Clanad is a hell of a lot more lenient than I am. Probably the first thing they'll do is to remove Bardot's pain."

"I'm not worried about Bardot," Quenby said. "You seem to be under a misapprehension about me. I don't like the idea of his suffering indefinitely, but he deserves some punishment. Men who victimize helpless children should never be let off scot-free."

"Then why are you so tense? I can practically feel the vibrations from here."

"Because I'm about to explode into a thousand pieces." Quenby drew a deep breath. "I want to talk to you." She turned and strode into the parlor, crossing to draw open the drapes and let the morning sunshine flood the room. She heard the front door close as Gunner followed her, but she didn't turn around.

"You're tired," Gunner said gently. "You went through hell last night and this morning and you're still upset about Steven. Why don't we postpone this talk until you've had some sleep?"

"Yes, I'm upset about Steven." Quenby carefully kept her voice controlled. "And about Andrew. And about this entire terrible mess." She whirled to face him, her eyes blazing. "But I'm mad as hell with you, Gunner!"

Gunner's eyes were suddenly wary. "I had to get Bardot, Quenby."

"Maybe you did, but you didn't have to do it alone. I think you've grown so accustomed to taking chances that it's become ingrained in you. Well, it's got to stop. I won't tolerate you risking your life." She paused. "Because it belongs to me."

He became still. "It does?"

She nodded. "You're damn right it does. Why do you think I came chasing down here after you? Your wonderful Clanad may put up with this guilt nonsense you're carrying like an albatross around your neck, but I have no intention—"

"Jon told you." Gunner frowned. "He shouldn't have done that. I wanted to tell you myself."

"If he'd left it up to you to tell me, I would probably have waited until hell froze over. You seem to think I shouldn't be burdened with any responsibilities heavier than which clothes to put on when I get out of bed in the morning. Remember what you said about both of us being caretakers and having to take turns? Well, you're not letting me have my turn. So I guess I'll just have to take it." She marched up to him and cradled his cheeks in her two hands. "You listen to me, Gunner Nilsen. You are *not* a freak. You're a wonderful, caring man with an amazing talent that you and your group use to help people. You're not responsible for your parents' deaths and you're not responsible for Andrew's problems. We all have to make choices and you made the best ones you could, given the facts you had. That's why there's not going to be any more guilt and there's certainly not going to be any more of this foolish risk-taking."

"No?" Gunner whispered, his gaze fixed intently on her face. "You seem to be very sure of that."

"I am sure."

"Why, Quenby?" Gunner asked softly. "Tell me why."

"Because I won't have it. Because you're my *valon*, dammit. Do you think I want the other half of me running around being shot at and walking tightropes and—"

He was kissing her, his arms crushing her with a force that took away her breath. He lifted his head. "You love me? You really love me?"

She blinked to keep back the tears that were stinging her eyes. "Oh, yes. Hell yes. I love you in every way I've ever thought it possible to love anyone. I love you with tenderness and passion, with my mind and my heart. I want to spend every minute of my life with you and I'll be damned if I let you cut short our life together. Every time you put yourself in any danger I'm going to be right behind you. No more chances, do you hear me?"

"I hear you." Gunner kissed her again. "How I love you, Quenby."

Her arms held him with fierce possession. "Then remember to let me be caretaker now and then. Let me love you and care for you. When you have a problem, talk to me, share with me."

"And you'll do the same?"

"Yes, I'll do the same." Her lips were trembling, but her eyes were glowing with a misty radiance. "I think I'll be pretty good at this *valon* business once I get the hang of it."

A tender smile touched Gunner's lips as he looked down at her. "You'll be a world-class *valon*, love. I'm so lucky you're mine." He chuckled. "And no one can say you don't pick original times to make your declarations. We're both exhausted, worried silly, and practically numb from everything that's happened."

A faint frown wrinkled her brow. "You think I chose the wrong time? I was so upset that—"

His fingers on her lips gently silenced her. "No, you chose the right time. There's no wrong time between people who love each other. That's what the *valon* is all about, a bond strong enough to endure the rough road as well as the smooth."

He drew her into his arms again and held her close. There was no passion in his embrace, just tenderness and a strength that wrapped her in warm security. She rested against him, her arms holding him with the same tenderness, giving peace and support to him as he was giving it to her.

She didn't know how long they stood there in the parlor holding each other in that magical closeness of spirit. It was a curiously timeless period, seeming to have no boundaries or tie to reality. They might have stood there indefinitely if the strident ring of the phone hadn't broken the spell.

Gunner's lips brushed her cheek. "I'll get it." He

released her, moved toward the phone in the foyer, and picked up the receiver. "Hello." Something flickered in his face. "Yes, Elizabeth."

Steven? A swift thrill of fear jarred Quenby from the serenity into which she had been lulled. She followed Gunner into the foyer, trying to read his expression as he listened to Elizabeth.

"You're sure?" he asked slowly. "I don't want to interfere."

What had happened? Quenby wondered. Was Steven . . . She wouldn't complete that thought even to herself.

"Good-bye, Elizabeth." Gunner hung up the phone.

"Steven?" Quenby's voice was charged with tension.

"Not good," Gunner said quietly. "He's still in a coma and they think his condition is worsening."

"Dear God," Quenby muttered, stricken.

"We have to get back to the hospital right away."

"They think it will be that soon?"

"No. It's Andrew," Gunner frowned. "Elizabeth says he's been acting very strangely for the past few hours. Remote, abstracted, self-absorbed. She's worried as hell about him." He took her arm and propelled her toward the front door. "He told her he wanted to talk to me. He's been very insistent about it."

"He loves you; it's natural that he'd want you with him now."

"Maybe." Gunner's expression was troubled as he opened the front door. "I guess we won't know until we see him."

• • •

Elizabeth met them in the corridor the moment they stepped off the elevator. "Lord, I'm glad you're here. I didn't know what to do. I've never seen Andrew like this."

"Where is he?" Gunner asked.

"In the waiting room with Jon." Elizabeth's slim, nervous hand grasped Gunner's arm. "I'm so frightened, Gunner. Andrew's never closed me out before."

"Then there must be a reason." Gunner covered her hand with his own, giving it a comforting squeeze. "Let's go see what it is."

Andrew was standing at the window, staring down at the parking lot below, when they walked into the waiting room. He turned to face them.

Quenby experienced a tiny shock as she gazed at Andrew. She had expected him to be distraught, but he appeared to be totally composed. His face was pale and shadows circled his eyes, but she did not see any evidence that he was feeling the wild, hopeless grief she had anticipated he might.

"Hello, Gunner." His endearingly hoarse voice was also calm. "I need to ask you a favor."

Jon Sandell rose from his chair and moved to stand beside Andrew. His hand rested on the child's shoulder. "You know we'll all do all we can to help, Andrew."

Andrew nodded. "I know. But you and Mama worry so about me. . . . You might bring me out too soon. Gunner loves me, too, but I think he'll let me stay until I've finished."

"What are you talking about, Andrew?" Elizabeth asked.

"I have to help Steven," Andrew said simply.

Gunner drew a swift, harsh breath and then strode across the room to drop to his knees beside Andrew. "Steven is—" He hesitated. "He's not doing well."

"He's dying," Andrew said clearly. "I can't let him die, Gunner. I have to do something."

Gunner's gaze searched Andrew's face. "What?"

"You said he was asleep and that he was having trouble willing himself to live because of the coma." Andrew gazed earnestly at Gunner. "I think I can wake him up. Steven is my friend. He'll let me come in."

Come in. Quenby felt a tiny thrill of fear. Those words could mean only one thing and Steven was *dying*. What would happen if Steven did die while Andrew was joined to him? "Andrew, you don't understand."

Andrew's gaze shifted to Quenby. "It's you who don't understand, Quenby. I can do this. Tell her, Gunner."

"He may be able to do it." Gunner's intent gaze never left Andrew's face. "Some of our best healers have been able to go in and reenforce the will to live in some cases." He paused. "But they've never been able to break through a coma, Andrew."

"No!" Elizabeth's voice was frantic with fear. "Jon, tell him what it might mean."

"We're both afraid you might—" Jon paused. "It might hurt you, Andrew. You've blocked out what you went through before, but if you could remember, you'd realize—"

"I do remember. I never really forgot, but I didn't want to let myself think about it." Andrew moistened his lips. "But I've been doing a lot of thinking since I've been sitting here." He drew a deep breath and his gaze shifted back to Gunner. "I'm scared, Gunner. I want you to help me. I don't want you to go in with me, but if you could sort of monitor and pull me out if—" He stopped and was silent a moment before continuing in a whisper. "I . . . I love him, Gunner. I'm afraid I might want to go with him."

Quenby felt Elizabeth, standing next to her, stiffen with an almost unbearable tension.

"Is it possible for you to do that?" Andrew asked.

"Yes, it's possible," Gunner said slowly.

"Andrew, I won't permit it." Elizabeth's voice was shaking.

"I don't want to disobey you, Mama." A flash of misery appeared on Andrew's face. "But I have to do it. I told Steven we would be friends forever and that would be long enough." His hands slowly clenched at his sides. "But it won't be long enough. Not if Steven dies." He looked at his mother. "If you won't let Gunner help me, I'll do it alone."

Elizabeth stood frozen, staring at him. The room was silent. Finally she spoke. "Andrew, I'm very much afraid I'm going to have problems with you." Her lips were trembling as she smiled at him. "You might have waited until you'd at least reached puberty before you lowered the boom on your poor old mother."

He smiled back at her. "I'll be all right, Mama."

"Of course you will. Gunner will see to that," Elizabeth said with great firmness. "Jon, you may have trouble getting permission from the doctor to let Andrew into Steven's room. Perhaps you'd better see about it."

"There won't be any objections," Jon said. "You're sure, Elizabeth?"

"I have to be." Elizabeth ran her fingers through her hair. "We have a major rebellion on our hands."

Jon nodded and said to Gunner, "Bring Andrew along in a few minutes. I'll make the arrangements." He turned and walked out of the waiting room and down the hall.

Gunner was speaking in a low voice to Andrew and the child was listening intently, nodding every now and then.

Were they planning some kind of strategy? Quenby wondered wildly. How did one formulate a strategy for a situation as bizarre as this?

She turned to Elizabeth and felt a sharp pang of sympathy. Elizabeth was staring at Andrew with a hunger that held desperation as well as resignation. Gunner had said Elizabeth was strong, but Quenby hadn't realized how strong until this moment. It must have taken great courage for her to give Andrew the support he needed rather than useless protests.

Quenby gently touched Elizabeth's arm. "Gunner won't let anything happen to him."

Elizabeth nodded. "That's what I keep telling myself. Who knows? It may all be for the best. At least Andrew has faced what traumatized him before and is willing to lower the barrier to help Steven." She bit her lip. "We don't know *anything* about this. What if—" She broke off as Andrew turned to face her. She smiled with an effort. "All set? Want me to go along?"

"No, I don't think so." Andrew ran across the room and into his mother's arms. "Mama, I . . ." He lifted his head and his eyes glittered with tears and a child's fear of the unknown. "I love you, Mama."

Elizabeth held him fiercely and then, slowly, released him. "Me too." She brushed his forehead with her lips. "I'll be waiting right here."

Quenby felt an aching desire to reach out and enfold Andrew in her arms as Elizabeth had done, but she could see that he was already fighting to resume his composure. She wouldn't risk weakening him now. "I'll keep your mother company," she said.

Andrew nodded gravely. "Thanks, Quenby."

Gunner crossed to stand beside him. "You can change your mind, Andrew. You don't have to do this."

"No, but I want to." He slipped his small hand into Gunner's big one. "Let's go, Gunner. This time I'm the one who's going to have the adventure."

Gunner smiled down at him. "Right."

They started toward the door.

"Andrew," Elizabeth called impulsively. She hesitated and then obviously substituted a question for the plea she had been about to make. "How are you going to do it? How are you going to help Steven?"

Andrew's smile lit his face with a radiance that appeared to hold both the wonder of a child and the wisdom of the ancients. "I'm going to show him his star."

Ten

Andrew and Gunner had been gone for a long time and the vigil Quenby and Elizabeth kept seemed to be extending into eternity.

"Can I get you something?" Quenby asked gently. "Coffee?"

Elizabeth shook her head. "Nothing." She smiled. "You're really getting a trial by fire, aren't you? It's not usually this rough, though I can't say we ever have a dull time of it in Sedikhan."

Quenby gazed at her thoughtfully. "But even when it's this rough, I don't think you'd change your life. It's all been worth it to you."

Elizabeth's smile was as radiant as her son's. "I've never regretted it for a single moment. Love makes all the difference."

Quenby felt she had a perfect understanding of Elizabeth. "Yes," she murmured, "love makes all the difference."

Jon walked into the waiting room and Quenby and Elizabeth stiffened in their chairs.

"Is it over?" Elizabeth asked.

"No," Jon said softly, "but I thought I'd give you a report. Steven's vital signs seem to be stabilizing." He paused and a slow smile lit his face. "And he just opened his eyes."

Elizabeth wilted in her chair. "Oh, thank God."

"Andrew and Gunner are still with him, but I think Steven is out of danger." Jon moved to stand before her. "I watched them for a while before I left to come to you and I probed a little." His hand reached out to stroke his wife's shining hair with infinite tenderness. "Andrew is exhausted, but he's holding on to Steven like a pup with a bone. He's not about to let him go and the things he's showing him are pretty wonderful. We have a very special son, Beth."

Elizabeth took his hand and held it against her cheek. "We always knew that, didn't we? Always."

Quenby quietly rose to her feet and moved toward the door. Elizabeth and Jon had no need of her. They had no need of anyone. They were wrapped in a closeness and love that encapsulated them in a world of their own. It was a very beautiful world, but it was not Quenby's world.

She started down the hall toward Steven's room, where her own world waited.

Where Gunner waited.

The night sky was blazing with stars.

Quenby nestled closer into the curve of Gunner's arm and sighed contentedly. It was a beautiful evening, warm and soft as the joyous warble of a nightingale and so like that other evening six weeks ago that she was experiencing a distinct feeling of déjà vu: The two of them gliding lazily on the porch swing, Steven and Andrew sitting on the bank of the stream looking at the stars, the soft liquid swoosh of the paddle wheel, the fireflies lighting the darkness.

"Something wrong?" Gunner asked, looking down at her.

She shook her head. "Something's right. No, everything's right. Lord, this is a wonderful place. I don't see how Elizabeth was able to leave it."

"She's happy in Sedikhan, but I think she did enjoy these last few weeks that she and Jon spent at Mill Cottage. When I took them to the airport this afternoon, she was a little quiet."

"I'm surprised she and Jon decided to leave Andrew and Steven here."

"It's only until the end of the summer, and Andrew and Steven are both making such progress here that Elizabeth and Jon didn't want to cause any disruption. They're healing each other, teaching each other."

"Yes." Quenby's gaze shifted to Andrew and Steven on the bank of the stream. "That's exactly what they're doing."

"And it gives me time to work with Andrew on forming a new protective barrier. Elizabeth decided she could survive without Andrew for another few months if it was for his own benefit."

"Survive," Quenby said out loud. "Yes, Elizabeth's definitely a survivor."

To her surprise, Gunner stiffened against her. "You think she'd have to be a survivor to be married to someone like Jon? Someone like me?"

She had unwittingly blundered into that very sensitive area of Gunner's insecurity, and she felt a swift jab of compunction. She was tempted to make an instant denial, but this was an issue that must be confronted. "Yes, she would," she said honestly. "And it's not going to be easy for me either to be married to someone with your talents. It's going to be exasperating and bewildering and I'm sure there'll be times when I'm going to throw up my hands and scream. And you'll probably feel the same way about me. I have faults just as you have. My plodding deliberations will probably cause you to climb the walls on occasion." She lifted her head from his shoulder to look him straight in the eye. "But every marriage has problems and every partner has to adjust and compromise. Our problems may not be the run-of-the-mill variety, but we'll survive. We have the magic ingredient."

Gunner's light eyes glittered in the moonlight. "And what's that?"

She smiled and leaned forward to kiss him gently. "Elizabeth said once that love made the difference. I think she's right."

Gunner nodded as he pressed her head back on his shoulder. His voice was oddly husky. "I think she is too. Lord, we're lucky, Quenby."

The silence that fell between them resonated with love and contentment as the porch swing glided slowly back and forth.

• • •

The fireflies fluttered in the darkness, the paddle wheel turned, the stars burned with white-hot brilliance. A man and a boy sat on the bank of the stream.

"Andrew, I learned that poem you gave me. Do you want to hear it?"

"Sure, Steven."

"Star Light, star bright
First star I see tonight
I wish I may, I wish I might
Have the wish, I wish tonight."

"That's super, Steven. You remembered every word."

"Do you think wishes really do come true?"

"I wouldn't be surprised."

"Do you suppose if I made a wish right now it would come true?"

"What would you wish for?"

"I don't know. . . . It's hard to think of much more to wish for right now. Maybe to have the fish bite when we go fishing tomorrow? Why are you laughing?"

"That's not a very big wish."

"Then I'll wish to catch a fish as big as a whale. Maybe a real whale."

"Let's leave the whales alone, Steven. They're having a pretty bad time of it as it is."

"Okay, then I'll wish we could get on a spaceship and go to my star."

"You know, I've been thinking about space travel and I'm not sure we'd want to go."

"Why not?"

"We'd have to leave a lot of people we love behind and, even if we were still young when we came back, they'd either be old or maybe even dead."

"If we were young, why wouldn't they still be young too?"

"It has to do with light speed and time. Einstein had a theory. . . . It's kind of complicated."

"I'd like to know."

"Would you? Okay, let me tell you about it." A pause. "No, there's a better way. . . ."

And while the stars shone down and the breeze whispered promises for tomorrow, Andrew showed him.

THE EDITOR'S CORNER

February is a favorite LOVESWEPT month. After all, it's the month dedicated to love and romance—and that's what we're all about! Romance is (and should be!) more important in our lives than just one special day, so LOVESWEPT is claiming February as a whole month dedicated to love. What a wonderful world it would be if we could convince everyone!

In this special month, we have six marvelous books with very pretty covers. In our LOVESWEPT Valentine month we have given all of our books covers in pink/red/purple shades—from pale pink confection, to hot fuschia pink, to red-hot-red, and passionate purple. This is our way of celebrating the month—so be sure to look for the SHADES OF LOVESWEPT covers, and we know you'll enjoy all the stories inside.

Our first book for the month, **STIFF COMPETITION,** LOVESWEPT #234, by Doris Parmett, is a heartwarming and very funny story about next door neighbors who are determined not to fall in love! Both Stacy and Kipp have been burned before and they go to ridiculous lengths to maintain their single status! But he can't resist the adorable vixen next door and she can't stop thinking of the devil-may-care hero of her dreams. When Kipp finally takes her in his arms, their resistance is swept away by sizzling passion and feel-

(continued)

ings telling them both that it's safe to trust again.

TOO HOT TO HANDLE, LOVESWEPT #235—This title tells all! Sandra Chastain's new book is full of sexy flirting, outrageous propositions, and hot pursuit. Matt Holland is a man after Callie Carmichael's classic convertible—or is it her cuddly, freckled body? Callie's not interested in any city slickers like Matt because she's a country girl living a free and easy life. But his kisses are too wonderful and they are bound to change her mind . . . and her lifestyle!

Next we have **SHARING SECRETS,** LOVESWEPT #236, by Barbara Boswell. We first met Rad Ramsey and Erin Brady in an earlier Barbara Boswell book, **PLAYING HARD TO GET,** which was a story about their siblings. Now Barbara has decided that Rad and Erin deserve a book of their own—and we agree! Sexy heartbreaker Rad knew women found him irresistible, but he'd always enjoyed the chase too much to keep the ladies whose hearts he captured. Erin had never known the fiery thrill of seduction, but Rad's touch awakened a woman who would be satisfied with nothing less. When they found each other, Rad knew he couldn't ignore his feelings and Erin knew she wanted this powerful, sensual, and loving man. This is a provocative story of a woman's first real passion and a man's true love.

Those incredible men surrounding Josh Logan are just fascinating, aren't they? Kay Hooper gives us another of the wonderful romances in what Carolyn Nichols calls the "Hagan Strikes Again Series" next month with **UNMASKING KELSEY,** LOVESWEPT #237. There is a terrible aura of fear hanging over the sleepy little town of Pinnacle, and beautiful Elizabeth Conner figures prominently in an episode that brings Kelsey there on the run and brings danger to a boil. Elizabeth also figures prominently in Kelsey's every thought, every dream . . . and she finds him utterly irresistible. This is one of Kay's most gripping and sensual romances and it seems to have "Don't You Dare Miss Me!" stamped all over it!

There's no more appealing Valentine story than
(continued)

MIDSUMMER SORCERY by Joan Elliott Pickart, Loveswept #238, an unforgettable story of first love—renewed. Fletcher McGill was back in town after six years and Nancy Forest was still furious at the man who captured her heart and then deserted her. They've been lonely difficult years and now Nancy is determined that Fletcher feel the full force of her hot anger—but instead, desire still flamed in her. Fletcher's touch scorched her, branded her with the heat that time and distance had never cooled. This time was his love as real and lasting as his passion?

We end the month with **THE PRINCE AND THE PATRIOT**, LOVESWEPT #239, a terrific book from Kathleen Creighton, a favorite LOVESWEPT author. This Valentine features a prince, some crown jewels, a European dynasty and a wonderful happy-ever-after ending. Our heroine, Willa Caris, is not a princess but a patriot. She's committed to protect the crown jewels of Brasovia, the small European country that was her parents' birthplace. Nicholas Francia is a prince in hiding and Willa doesn't know the truth behind his playboy facade. Carried away by tempestuous desire, Nicholas and Willa surrender to their intense attraction and need for one another . . . believing that the goals in their "real" lives are at odds. When the surprising truth is revealed, their love for each other proves to be as strong as their love for their traditions.

Remember to look for the six Valentine covers and spend the month in love—with LOVESWEPT!

Sincerely,

Kate Hartson

Kate Hartson
  Editor
LOVESWEPT
Bantam Books, Inc.
666 Fifth Avenue
New York, NY 10103

The first Delaney trilogy

Heirs to a great dynasty, the Delaney brothers were united by blood, united by devotion to their rugged land . . . and known far and wide as

THE SHAMROCK TRINITY

Bantam's bestselling LOVESWEPT romance line built its reputation on quality and innovation. Now, a remarkable and unique event in romance publishing comes from the same source: THE SHAMROCK TRINITY, three daringly original novels written by three of the most successful women's romance writers today. Kay Hooper, Iris Johansen, and Fayrene Preston have created a trio of books that are dynamite love stories bursting with strong, fascinating male and female characters, deeply sensual love scenes, the humor for which LOVESWEPT is famous, and a deliciously fresh approach to romance writing.

THE SHAMROCK TRINITY—Burke, York, and Rafe: Powerful men . . . rakes and charmers . . . they needed only love to make their lives complete.

☐ *RAFE, THE MAVERICK* by Kay Hooper

Rafe Delaney was a heartbreaker whose ebony eyes held laughing devils and whose lilting voice could charm any lady—or any horse—until a stallion named Diablo left him in the dust. It took Maggie O'Riley to work her magic on the impossible horse . . . and on his bold owner. Maggie's grace and strength made Rafe yearn to share the raw beauty of his land with her, to teach her the exquisite pleasure of yielding to the heat inside her. Maggie was stirred by Rafe's passion, but would his reputation and her ambition keep their kindred spirits apart?   (21846 • $2.75)

LOVESWEPT

☐ YORK, THE RENEGADE by Iris Johansen

Some men were made to fight dragons, Sierra Smith thought when she first met York Delaney. The rebel brother had roamed the world for years before calling the rough mining town of Hell's Bluff home. Now, the spirited young woman who'd penetrated this renegade's paradise had awakened a savage and tender possessiveness in York: something he never expected to find in himself. Sierra had known loneliness and isolation too—enough to realize that York's restlessness had only to do with finding a place to belong. Could she convince him that love was such a place, that the refuge he'd always sought was in her arms?

(21847 • $2.75)

☐ BURKE, THE KINGPIN by Fayrene Preston

Cara Winston appeared as a fantasy, racing on horseback to catch the day's last light—her silver hair glistening, her dress the color of the Arizona sunset . . . and Burke Delaney wanted her. She was on his horse, on his land: she would have to belong to him too. But Cara was quicksilver, impossible to hold, a wild creature whose scent was midnight flowers and sweet grass. Burke had always taken what he wanted, by willing it or fighting for it; Cara cherished her freedom and refused to believe his love would last. Could he make her see he'd captured her to have and hold forever?

(21848 • $2.75)

The Delaney Dynasty Lives On!

The Bestselling Creators Of The Shamrock Trinity Bring You Three More Sizzling Novels

The Delaneys of Killaroo

Daring women, dreamers, and doers, they would risk anything for the land they loved and the men who possessed their hearts.